LOVING MY OMEGA

C.W. GRAY

TANGLEWOOD PRESS

CONTENTS

"*D*aniella said the manager position is mine if I want it." Sam shifted the grocery bags in his arms and opened the door to his apartment building. "I just don't know if I want it."

"You love cooking." Teague's voice was deep and clear against Sam's ear, as if he were standing right beside him, instead of speaking through Sam's Bluetooth.

"I really do." Sam sighed. "The position pays more, but I won't have as much time back in the kitchen."

"It doesn't sound right for you."

Sam bit his lip. "Brett says that if I'm not going to go to culinary school, then there's no point working in the kitchen, when I can make more money at the front of a restaurant."

"Brett's a fucking idiot." Teague's low growl in his ear sent a shiver down Sam's back. His best friend had the absolute *best* voice in the whole world. He could be as comforting as a warm, fuzzy blanket on a cold day, or as sexy as a phone-sex operator.

"He's just thinking of our future," Sam said, shuffling bags again to hunt for his keys. "I'm thinking that's why he hasn't proposed yet. I don't blame him for wanting to have all our ducks in a row before we take that final step."

Teague grunted. "I know you love the guy, but he *is* a fucking idiot. You've been together for over five years. I would have locked that shit down with a ring on your finger by now."

Sam flushed, happy his friend couldn't see him. He took it way too personally when Teague said things like that. The alpha was just being supportive, but sometimes, late at night, when he was by himself, Sam thought about what would have happened if he had met Teague before Brett.

"I have a feeling this is the year it's going to happen." Sam unlocked the door and pushed it open. "Brett and I are in a really good place, so I'm thinking a huge, fancy proposal is—"

Sam stared at the suitcases and boxes filling the entry. He recognized his favorite pillow on top of one of the stacks.

"Sam?" Teague cursed softly. "Did the fucking phone cut out?"

"Something's not right," Sam whispered, shaking himself.

He stepped around the stacks and looked for Brett. He found him working in his home office. His alpha worked from home a lot even when he wasn't in the office. Sam tried to get him to take a break more often, but Brett was a bit of a workaholic.

Sam eyed the new desk in front of the window, wondering why Brett needed a second desk. "Hey, why are my things packed up in the entry?"

Brett spun his chair around and blinked, mind clearly still on the screen in front of him. He was still dressed in his work suit, but his jacket was on the back of the chair, and his tie loosened around his neck.

Brett winced and grabbed his phone. "Shit. I forgot to text you at lunch, didn't I?"

"Sam, what's going on?" Teague asked, voice full of concern.

"What were you going to text me at lunch?" Sam asked, voice small. He was used to Brett's distance when he was working, but the coldness in his alpha's eyes was a bit worrying.

"I didn't want to have to deal with this." Brett groaned and stood up, working the kinks out of his shoulders and back. "I need you out of the apartment tonight, so I had a service come and pack your things. Don't worry, I gave them a list, so everything should be there."

"What do you mean you need me out of the apartment?" Sam suddenly wished he hadn't eaten a late lunch of clam chowder. His hands shook as he twisted his keys in his fingers.

Brett gave him an annoyed look. "Do I really need to say it? I met someone else. Martin works in the office building next to mine. He's a lawyer, Sam. He actually has ambition. He's moving in tomorrow."

"What?" Sam hated the tears he heard in his voice. "You're *my* alpha."

This isn't happening. I got hit by a car walking home and am dreaming. It's just a nightmare.

Brett groaned and ran his hands through his hair. "You're so small-town omega. I can't even deal with you right now. Just get your things out before tomorrow morning."

"I'm on my way over." Teague's deep voice was a dash of reality, breaking through the fog filling Sam's mind. "Be there in five minutes."

"Brett, we've been together since college." Sam swallowed hard, looking around for something to help him understand what was happening. "This is just a joke, right?"

"I'm sorry you're so upset, Sam." Brett gently turned Sam around and pushed him out of the office. "Look at it from my point of view. I'm a rising star at the investment firm, and you're a fine-arts graduate, working at a restaurant. Martin and I make sense. You and I are the real joke."

Sam turned around, cheeks wet from his tears. "This is really happening? We were fine this morning."

"Martin hadn't agreed to move in this morning," Brett said, crossing his arms. "We can still be friends, Sam. Hell, we've been together for years. It would be strange not having you to talk to. I'll call you tomorrow, okay?"

He didn't wait for an answer and firmly shut the office door.

Sam heard the lock engage.

He stood there, staring at the closed door, until he heard Teague's familiar curses from the front of the apartment.

Sam slowly turned and walked away.

Teague stood amongst all of Sam's things. His friend was a large man, with warm, brown skin he'd inherited from his Guatemalan omega grandfather. His sharply angled face, and wide, muscular shoulders came from his Scottish alpha grandfather. Teague's dad, Timothy, always told Sam that Teague looked more like Timothy's parents than he did.

Random thoughts. Sam shifted from foot to foot and stared around the small entry. The apartment was impeccably decorated and as cold and formal as always. There had been very little of him outside of the bedroom, so it probably hadn't been hard for the movers to pack up his things. *Always cold,* he thought, shivering.

"Sammie." Teague gave him a sympathetic look and opened his arms. "Come here."

Sam ran to him and settled into the hug. Teague's strong arms and comforting scent eased some of Sam's rising panic. "He's moving someone named Martin in tomorrow."

"Fucker was cheating on you?" Teague's voice got louder, and he started to let go of Sam. "Where is he at?"

Sam's body started shaking, and he clung tighter to his friend. "Don't leave. Please. Just help me. I don't want to be here anymore."

"Then, we'll get you out of here." Teague rubbed his hands up and down Sam's bare arms. "I'll get you settled at that corner diner you like so well, then I'll come and get your things. This may all fit in the back of my Jeep."

Sam nodded, burying his face against Teague's chest. "I want meatloaf."

Teague chuckled. "Comfort food it is. Come on, Sammie. This place is shit anyway. You couldn't even bring Morris here."

"Brett doesn't like animals," Sam whispered, wiping his cheeks. He kept a strong hold on Teague's hand and let his friend lead him out of the apartment.

"Luckily, you do," Teague said, smiling. "The herd will be happy to have you around."

"I can stay with you?" he asked, voice sounding as pathetic as he felt.

"Of course, you're staying with me." Teague squeezed his hand. "What are best friends for?"

TEAGUE HAD a nice home with a small fenced-in backyard in one of Seattle's many suburbs. Teague had once told Sam that he didn't mind the commute to his veterinary clinic, not when it meant he could have his herd.

The curtains moved and a familiar, white, fuzzy face grinned at him. Moose was a Great Pyrenees, and one of Sam's favorites.

Teague unlocked his door, and called out, "We're back, Mrs. Darnell."

"Oh, Sammie. You poor thing." Mrs. Darnell unburied

herself from Teague's many cats and dogs and stood up. "I never liked that alpha of yours. He was too snooty if you ask me."

Mrs. Darnell had only met Brett once, but he had left an impression since he'd run from Teague's house, screaming about the demon bird that wanted to eat him.

"Dinner," Binks, Teague's grey and yellow Cockatiel, said from his perch near the door.

"He would have made a nasty dinner, Binky," Mrs. Darnell said, snickering. "I'll let you boys settle in. If you need anything, Sam, let me know."

"Thanks for pet-sitting, Mrs. Darnell." Teague bent and kissed her cheek. "You're a treasure."

Their conversation faded to the background as Sam sat on the couch and was instantly swarmed by dogs and cats. Moose panted next to his ear and settled a massive paw on Sam's stomach.

Orville, Teague's miniature pig, grunted from the floor, and Sam felt him settle on top of his feet.

"This doesn't feel real," Sam whispered. "What the hell am I without Brett? I've loved him for years, Moose. Things weren't always perfect, but he was mine."

He closed his eyes and memories rushed forward. The day he and Brett had met on campus. The first time they had kissed. The first time they'd made love. Sam remembered bringing him home to meet Aunt Mia in Hobson Hills. His aunt hadn't liked Brett much either, but she was polite and had given him a chance.

He remembered Brett's laughter as they watched one of their favorite, classic, romantic comedies. The feel of Brett's arm around his shoulders.

The words Brett had whispered as he pounded into Sam from behind. *I love you so much, my sweet omega.*

"How can this be real if *that* was real?" Sam asked, burying his face in Lilly's fur. The fuzzy brown dog wiggled in his lap, happy to be near him.

"Meow." Charlie, Teague's three-legged black cat, batted at Sam's face.

Teague rubbed the cat's head, then sighed and collapsed against Moose. "Day from hell, guys. Day from hell."

"My love." Morris flew into the room from the hallway. "My one true love."

Sam laughed when the African Grey Parrot landed on Moose's head. He gently picked the bird up and helped him perch on his fingers. "Here I am, my love. I missed you too."

Teague chuckled and snapped a picture. "I'm sending this to Dad. He's upset that he's not here to hug you right now."

"You already texted Timothy?" Sam asked.

Teague shrugged, eyes on his phone. "Dad hates that he hasn't met you yet. Without Brett monopolizing your time, it'll be easier to arrange dinner next time Dad's in town."

"I love him already." Sam stroked a finger down Morris's back. "We talk weekly. He asks my opinion on everything, especially whatever man's in your life at the time. He likes Dorian a little bit. A lot better than the last one, really."

Teague rolled his eyes. "Dads can be nosy as hell." He smirked. "I guess I can't be too judgy. I talk to Aunt Mia every week too. She really doesn't like Brett, just so you know."

Sam grunted. "I'm aware."

His phone vibrated in his pocket, and he dug around until he found it. He frowned when he saw the number. It was a lot later in Hobson Hills than Seattle. "Aunt Mia? Why are you calling so late? Is something wrong?"

Sam listened to his great-aunt, his mind scattering at the word *cancer*. Sam didn't know what Teague saw in his expression, but whatever it was must have worried him.

Teague shuffled animals around, until he could sit next to Sam and wrap him in his arms.

"The doctors are sure?" Sam asked, tears filling his eyes for the second time that night. "It's cancer?"

Teague cursed and squeezed him tight.

"I'll be there as soon as possible." Sam met his friend's gaze, recognizing the panic and worry he saw reflected in them. "We can handle this, Aunt Mia. No problem."

CHAPTER 2

SIX MONTHS LATER

"We had a nice night, even if there was zero romance involved." Sam sounded happy over the phone, which should have made Teague happy.

"It's only been six months since you and Brett broke up." Teague scowled, hating to even say the fucker's name. "Are you ready to be dating again?"

"Not at all," Sam said with a laugh. "That's why I'm letting my boss set me up with Zed. The alpha is crazy about his friend Noah, so there is no way he's going to expect anything from me. It's just really nice to get out right now. I haven't had a lot of free time." A mix of emotions filled his voice. "It's been hard, Tee."

Teague instantly felt guilty for saying anything. "How's Aunt Mia?"

"The chemo treatments take a lot out of her." Sam sighed heavily. "I expected the fatigue, but I didn't realize how much it would mess with her appetite. She used to love eating, but now she'll only eat peanut-butter toast, and occasionally, some oatmeal. That's it. She's lost so much weight and looks like she'll break apart if I touch her. I'm about ready to force-feed her."

"Have they scheduled her surgery yet?" Teague leaned back in his chair, hating the walls of his familiar office. They were keeping him from Sam.

"The doctor says that he wants to do two more cycles of chemo, then see where we are."

Teague scratched at the wooden desktop. "She's eighty-two, Sam. Can she handle two more cycles of chemo and a surgery?"

Sam sniffed, voice full of tears. "She has to. Aunt Mia's not ready to die. She said she'd fight."

"For you," Teague whispered.

"I need her." Sam's voice got higher as he tried not to cry. "She's all the family I have. Who will call me peanut, sweet potato, or tater tot? Hell, I'll even take being called donut hole, and that one really confuses me. You and Aunt Mia are the only people on this planet that love me. I can't lose either one of you."

"And I'm all the way across the country." Teague rolled his shoulders, trying to ease the tension that had been weighing on him every day that Sam had been gone. "I think I should come help."

"Fuck, I want to say get on a plane tonight, but you can't." Sam huffed. "You can't drop your life just because I'm feeling whiny. Your clinic needs you, and you should be looking for places for the animal rescue sanctuary. You don't have time to come here and hold my damn hand."

Doesn't mean I don't want to, Teague thought, leaning his head back and staring at the ceiling. "I hate that you're in Maine and I'm in Washington."

"Me too, but it's temporary." Sam laughed harshly. "Brett calls me every week. Who knows? Maybe by the time Aunt Mia's on her feet again, Brett and I will be back together."

Teague scowled and spun his chair around, so he could look out the window. "Do you really want that?"

Sam was quiet for a moment. "I don't know. I want it to be like it was when I first met Brett. We had so many plans and were happy. I don't think I could forgive the cheating though."

"You deserve better than him," Teague said, voice gravelly. Sometimes he wished he could have known Sam before his friend had met Brett. He could have warned him away from the asshole.

"It's not like he wants me anyway." Sam scoffed. "He sent me links to engagement rings for my opinion. He's going to propose to Martin."

Teague sat up in his chair. "That piece of shit really did that? How does he think that's going to make you feel?"

"I don't think he cares." Sam sounded tired. "My lunch break is almost over, and I've depressed you enough for your morning. Face chat tonight?"

"Of course." Teague rubbed his face. "You know Morris needs to see you."

"My pretty bird," Sam said softly, a smile in his voice. "You got breakfast, didn't you?"

Teague looked at the uneaten muffin sitting on his desk. "Yeah."

"Don't skip your own lunch today. Promise you won't forget."

Teague smiled. "I promise, I'll eat lunch."

"Okay. I love you."

"Love you too, donut hole." Teague took the Bluetooth from his ear and set it on his desk. His first patient of the day would arrive in an hour, and he still needed to do inventory.

Normally, he loved all the mundanities involved in owning his own veterinary clinic, but lately nothing seemed to make him happy. Nothing, except talking to Sam.

He stood up and checked on Tortellini. His tortoise came with him to the clinic often, so he had his own terrarium set up in front of the window. On warmer days, Teague let him wander around the office.

Teague watched Tortellini munch his way through a plate of mustard and collard greens. "I miss, Sam. I know how he feels. Dad and Sam are the only ones walking this planet that love me too. It's a lonely place to be sometimes, Tort. Dorian's nice and all, but we aren't at the love stage yet. Sam has friends in Hobson Hills too, but it's not the same."

Tortellini ignored him and focused on the little sliver of bell pepper that Teague had hidden within the greens.

"Still, I shouldn't miss him this much, should I?" Teague asked. "Dorian says I shouldn't, but all I can think about is getting home, so I can face chat with Sam."

Tortellini started nosing around the kiwi slices on the edge of the plate.

Teague smiled. "You don't care, do you?"

"Dr. Walsh?" Katie cracked his door. "We have an emergency. A stray dog was hit by a car two blocks over. The driver brought the poor fella in. He's a mess."

"On my way," Teague said, shoving the thought of Sam from his mind.

LATER THAT NIGHT, Teague sat on the couch and watched his favorite post-apocalyptic zombie show on the television. The frozen dinner he'd eaten sat funny on his stomach, but that could be due to the pit bull sprawled across his lap. Percy had no sense of boundaries, and his gray head was wedged right against Teague's gut.

Binks whistled loudly from where he sat atop Teague's

head, and Orville and all the dogs stood up, tails wagging as they surrounded the couch.

"No treats," Teague said, voice firm. "That was Binks, and we all know he's a shithead. Ignore him."

They weren't convinced.

Teague groaned and reached for the treat jar that sat on the side table for this exact reason. "Go play with the cats, Binks."

As he passed out treats, his bird hopped from his head to the arm of the couch.

Binks let out a convincing *meow*.

Noodle, Teague's thin Siamese cat, gave the bird a disinterested look before she continued cleaning her paws.

Teague chuckled. "No wonder you'd rather play with the dogs."

Percy and the other dogs settled back down, and Teague checked the time on his phone. It was too late to call Sam again, but it was too early to go to bed.

He sighed and tried to focus on the show. *Fuck the humans, but I swear if that dog dies, I'm never watching this show again.*

Teague looked around at his herd. He didn't bother counting everyone. His philosophy was that if he never admitted to himself how many pets he had, he could never have too many.

"Guys, I'll never abandon you in a zombie apocalypse, okay? Binks may get us all killed with his antics, but we'll die together."

Percy reached up and licked his chin, and Charlie purred from where the cat curled against his leg.

Teague loved his pets, and they sure eased a lot of his loneliness with Sam gone. "Sam and I will take you all and go live on an island somewhere with Aunt Mia." Teague thought about it a moment. "I'd have to call him as soon as things went to shit though. We'll have to meet somewhere and pick an island."

The squeak of Barnaby's wheel filled the silence. The hamster got on the damn thing every evening and stayed on it until morning.

Teague licked his lips. "It would be hard getting to Sam and Aunt Mia. Guys, I don't know if I could do a zombie apocalypse without Sam."

Life was hard without Sam. Teague could imagine his friend sitting in his usual spot on the other side of the couch as they did a movie marathon. Sam had loved cooking in Teague's kitchen and made the best chicken parmesan. He had the best sense of humor and didn't seem to mind Teague's occasional—okay, the right word would be *usual* —grumpiness.

Sam also loved Teague's herd as much as he did. That was something Dorian couldn't deal with. He didn't want so many animals underfoot all the time, and he had issues with one of them.

Teague eyed Orville. The miniature pig curled up with Lily on one of the large dog beds. "You really shouldn't torture Dorian. He can't help that he doesn't realize how magnificent you are."

Teague picked his phone back up and did a search for animal sanctuaries in Maine. Most of the ones he saw were on the coast, but Hobson Hills was inland and farther north.

He tossed his phone on the side table. "Sam will be back in a few months. It's no big deal. We'll survive. Right guys?"

Noodle watched him steadily.

"I need more sponsors for the sanctuary anyway," Teague said, slipping farther down in the couch. "Plus, there's my clinic to think about. Oh, and Dorian, I guess. He *is* my boyfriend."

Moose's deep snores drowned out the television.

"Don't worry. I'm not going to move us all across the country or anything." Teague frowned and hugged Percy. "Sam's not really dating that alpha he told me about. Aunt Mia will get better, and Sam will come home. He can move into my guest room with Puff and Tortellini. Everything's going to be just fine."

CHAPTER 3

SIX MONTHS LATER

Sam chuckled and settled into the mound of pillows covering his bed. His computer balanced on his lap, and his best friend's grumpy face filled the screen. Teague's brown hair stood on end, and his sharply angled face looked almost demonic. Binks nestled on top of his head.

"Why are you wearing your grumpy and annoyed face?" Sam asked, scratching at the scruff covering his cheeks.

"A client called the clinic today and yelled at Katie." Teague scowled and rubbed his hands over his face. "He claimed the flea medicine we'd recommended was making his dog foam at the mouth."

Sam winced. "Shit, I thought this was your annoyed face, not your upset face. Is the dog okay?"

Teague arched a brow and pointed at his face. "Oh, this is my annoyed face. Katie asked him a few more questions and found out that the dumbass put the *topical* flea shampoo in Snoopy's food. Luckily, the pooch will be okay, but I swear, sometimes, I want to do really bad things to people."

Sam shook his head. "Didn't he read the directions on the bottle? People make me wonder sometimes."

Binks whistled, sounding eerily like Teague's cell phone.

"Binks agrees." Teague blew out a loud breath and rolled his shoulders. "Tell me good things. How did Aunt Mia's checkup go?"

Sam's smile was wide enough to make his face hurt. "Cancer free."

The grumpiness disappeared from his friend's face as joy filled Teague's brown eyes. Teague had the best smile in the whole world, partly because it was so rare.

"That's great." Teague pumped his arms in the air and whooped loudly. Binks leaned his body into Teague's movements, keeping his perch, but Sam heard an unhappy meow before he saw Noodle stalk across the screen. The thin Siamese cat was disgruntled-grace personified.

"Don't upset her highness." Sam snickered when Noodle paused to give him a look of disdain. He heard a squawk in the background, quickly followed by grunting. "Is Orville picking on my sweet Morris again?"

Teague rolled his eyes. "Orville is just protecting himself. There's nothing sweet about that bird unless you're here." He narrowed his eyes. "Speaking of, when are you coming home? If Aunt Mia is good to go, then she doesn't need you anymore, right?"

Sam's smile slowly faded away, and the almost ever-present, overwhelming numbness was back. "She's still recovering from the last chemo treatment, Teague. Plus, I don't think she needs to be on her own. Not at her age."

Teague tilted his head, Binks leaning with him. "Your aunt wouldn't want you to put your life on hold for her. Taking care of her has been hard for you."

"It's been harder on her, so I can deal. I love her." Sam frowned and looked away from the screen. The past year had been emotionally and physically exhausting, but his aunt was alive and doing well, all things considered.

Teague's voice softened. "I may have only video chatted with her, but I know Mia would be the first one to tell you that you need to take care of yourself too. Now, be honest with me. Why don't you seem eager to come home? When Mia called you last year, you didn't seem upset to leave Seattle."

Sam bit his lip. "You know why I wanted to leave."

Teague growled. "He didn't deserve your love, Sam."

"That doesn't mean that he didn't have it," Sam whispered, cheeks heating. "We were together for years, and I followed Brett all the way to Seattle. You know how well that worked out."

Sam hated being a cliché—the omega that followed his boyfriend across the country just to be dumped for a younger man. *At least I wasn't the omega that ended up pregnant and dumped,* he thought grumpily.

"When Aunt Mia called I wasn't thinking of anyone but her, but I have to admit it didn't exactly hurt to leave Brett and his new omega behind."

Teague gave him an exasperated look. "I get it, but it's been a year. It's time to think of your own needs. You deserve to have someone that adores you. Not someone like Brett that takes advantage of you over and over again. Besides, Brett and that Martin guy have moved on. So should you."

Sam blinked, trying to keep the tears from falling. Brett and his younger—and much more successful—boyfriend had gotten married last month. It had hurt, but not as much as Sam had thought it would. A year was a long time, and Teague had been with him every step of the way, even if he was far away.

"Shit, I'm sorry, Sammie. I shouldn't have said all that." Teague gave him a pained look. "I mean it, but I didn't have to throw it all in your face."

Sam took a deep breath and let it out. "No, I know you're

right. That's why I've been going on a few more blind dates. I went out with an alpha friend of Abel's last night."

Teague's scowl returned. "You're dating? For real this time, not like those dates with that Zed guy?"

Sam gave him a look, baffled. "I thought you would approve."

The alpha shook his head, hard. "You need to come home."

Sam nibbled his lip, a surprising reluctance filling him. He didn't want to leave Hobson Hills, but he wanted to see Teague again. They talked every night, but it was different. When he lived in Seattle, they went out all the time, or hung out at Teague's house.

Sam closed his eyes. "I turn thirty in a few months, and you said it, Teague, I need my own life. The best way to do that is to let the past go. The only good thing about Seattle is you and the herd."

Teague made a pained noise, and Sam's eyes flew open.

He hated upsetting Teague. They had met three years ago, and it was Teague that made Sam realize the traits he had thought were *quirky* in Brett, were actually just selfishness. Brett prided himself on speaking his mind and not taking shit from other people, when, in reality, he just liked doing and saying what he wanted without considering other people.

"I don't want to leave you," Sam said, voice soft. "I just need Hobson Hills right now."

Binks gave Sam a sad birdie look, as Teague's shoulders slumped. "I want to tell you to come back here for me, but you're right. You've never really been happy here. I know you've missed your hometown."

Sam wiped his eyes. "I'm a small-town kind of man. Aunt Mia wants to move into the in-law suite at the back of the house and sign everything over to me. It's either that or she wants to move to the retirement community the next town over."

"Keep her with you as long as you can," Teague said, shaking his head.

Sam nodded, his smile strained. "I'm going to remodel the house. You saw those pictures I sent of the kitchen, right?"

Teague shuddered. "That wallpaper haunts me, and who puts shag carpet in *their kitchen?*"

Sam laughed, wiping the rest of his tears on one of his pillows. "I know, right? You'll have to help me pick out new flooring."

"I'll start looking online." Teague reached down and pulled Charlie into his lap. "You know I like home improvement sites."

"Oh, that reminds me. How is Project Animal Sanctuary going?" Sam snuggled down deeper into his pile of pillows. "Did you get that big sponsor?"

"Since the big sponsor is my dad, yes. Yes, I did," Teague said dryly. "Dad is willing to back the sanctuary. I'm just looking for property. I have my own money to invest too, and the clinic is turning a profit."

Sam wiggled in place. "I can just see you surrounded by rescued animals."

Teague looked around him. "If you were here, you'd see that now."

"Is Dorian getting along any better with the herd?" Sam asked, laughing as he remembered the picture Teague had sent him of his boyfriend running away from Orville. Apparently, the omega was afraid of miniature pigs. Sam probably shouldn't have been happy about that.

Teague gave him a guilty look. "Don't be mad."

Sam eyed his screen. "Nothing good comes from a conversation that starts with those words."

Teague made a face and reached up to run a finger over

Binks's back. "I should have told you, but it was no big deal, and I knew you'd make it into a big deal."

"What?" Sam asked, intrigued.

"Dorian and I broke up a while ago."

Sam tried to stifle the happiness he felt at those words. "I'm sorry. I know you really liked him."

Teague shrugged. "It was a mutual breakup. He didn't think I should adopt another dog, but Nugget needed me."

"Wait, you have a new dog and haven't introduced him to me? I'm disappointed in you, Tee. You've been holding out on me." Sam gave him an exasperated look. "Dorian may have had a point though. That makes five dogs."

"I didn't hear that." Teague whistled, and Binks did the same, mimicking his person. "Nugget, come here, sweet boy."

A moment later, the fuzzy face of a golden retriever filled the screen. The dog had a giraffe hat strapped onto his head.

"This is Nugget," Teague said, running his hands over the dog's hat. "He apparently has a thing for hats. He picks one out each morning and wears it all day. He had to have surgery on his tail to remove some cancerous tumors, and his previous owner didn't want to bother. He was just going to put Nugget down."

Sam cooed at the screen. "You poor sweet boy. Did your new daddy sweep in and save you? He's the bestest vet in the whole world. Yes, he is."

A pang of grief hit him suddenly. He wanted to be there to help Teague pick out property for the sanctuary. He wanted to visit his friend every night and hug and love on the man's many, many pets.

The knowledge that Teague was single again, especially now that Sam was too, was giving him ideas that he was best off ignoring.

"Can I talk to Morris?" he asked, struggling to smile.

"Of course. Your bird misses you." Teague hugged Nugget, then stood.

"He's not my bird," Sam said, his smile coming a little easier.

Teague settled the African Grey Parrot on the back of his chair.

Morris cocked his head and ruffled his feathers. "Hey, beautiful."

Sam smiled. "Hello, my love. I miss you."

THE NEXT MORNING, Sam watched his great aunt sip her coffee, smiling at the look of bliss on her face. "Good?"

"Mmmhmm," she said, taking another sip. "Zoe makes the best coffee."

"I brought you a breakfast pastry too." Sam yawned behind his hand and went to grab a plate.

The clash of colors in Aunt Mia's kitchen made him wince. Puke-green Formica counters sat atop thin, particle-board wooden cabinets, clashing horribly with the wildly patterned wallpaper. Everything was clean and orderly, but the room—hell, the whole house really—could use an update.

"What time do you go to work today?" Mia asked, smacking her lips happily when he handed her a plate with Zoe's bacon, egg, and cheese pastry on it.

"Ten. I'll work until six tonight." He sat across from her and grinned. "I already asked for time off for the next doctor's appointment. Four months until you need to see a doctor again. I knew they were optimistic after the surgery, but I swear I almost fell out of my chair yesterday when Dr. Millard said you were good."

Mia smiled, eyes dancing. "You *did* trip walking out the door, sweet potato."

His aunt had always been larger than life to him. She was in her early eighties now, but until the past year, she hadn't looked her age. *Cancer has a way of fucking things up*, he thought. Chemo treatments had taken their toll of the vibrant woman, but she was still his Aunt Mia, the woman who had raised him when his parents died.

"Stop looking at me like that," she said, rolling her eyes. "You're getting all weepy, and it's embarrassing."

Sam sniffled, then hurried around the table to hug her thin frame. "I don't want to lose you."

Mia sighed and patted his back. "I'm not going anywhere, sweetie. Now, you never told me how the date went last weekend." She gave him a sad look. "Do an old lady a solid and tell her every ridiculous detail."

Sam made a face and returned to his seat. "How do you know it was ridiculous?"

She arched a brow. "You've been hurting over that asswipe ex of yours, and now you have a handsome, kind alpha keeping you up on video calls all night. You have just a wee bit of baggage, tater tot. How could any date be something other than ridiculous?"

Sam smoothed a hand over the rattan placemat in front of him, and did his best not to think of either Brett or Teague. "I had a lovely time with Daryl."

She stared at him, waiting patiently like the horrible spider aunt she was.

"I hate you." He sighed and slumped down in his chair. "Daryl was nice, but there just wasn't any spark. We even kissed, but it was like kissing a ham."

Mia snorted a laugh. "Is that what you do at work? Spend your time kissing the hams in the freezer?"

"I really do hate you." Sam laughed, and leaned back in his chair. "Guess what Tee told me last night?"

"That he's madly in love with you and wants to give you a

million babies?" Mia grinned and waggled her eyebrows, then snorted. "Don't look at me like that. I know he's dating that man you told me about."

Sam turned off his stink eye and leaned across the table. "Not anymore. They broke up, because the horrible, cold-hearted monster wanted Teague to turn away a sweet dog that needed his help."

"The bastard," Mia gasped theatrically, pressing her hand to her chest.

"I know, right?" He stole a piece of her pastry.

"Maybe you should move back to Seattle and Teague," Mia said, eyes softening. "I love having you here, but that is one fine man, and you're young enough to enjoy him. You both haven't been single at the same time since you met. This is a sign, peanut."

Sam shook his head hard, refusing to even contemplate Teague as a lover rather than a friend. *Except when I'm alone in bed, or taking a shower,* he mentally amended. "No, no, no. Teague is my best friend, Aunt Mia. He's never given any sort of indication that he wants more than that with me."

"That's because you're both idiots," Mia said, pulling a piece from her pastry and popping it in her mouth. "I just don't want you pining after him like you do for Brett the Giant Dillweed."

"First, I'm not pining after Brett," Sam said, scowling. "I'm moving on. Second, Teague isn't an idiot. He has a very successful veterinarian clinic, and he's a doctor, Aunt Mia. *A doctor.*"

"An animal doctor." Mia shook her head and gave him a knowing look. "Besides, there are different kinds of intelligence, sweet pea, and I can tell you that both of you boys need a good smack of common sense right atop your heads."

Sam sighed and stood. "Please just stop. Teague is the absolute best person I know, and I'm not going to fuck up our friendship by trying to push for more." *Even if I want to lick him all over.*

Mia made a face. "If I was just a few years younger, I'd fight you for him."

"A few years younger?" Sam asked, arching a brow and grabbing his car keys from the counter. "Then you'd be in your seventies, old woman. Go chase Mr. Spencer down the street."

Mia chuckled. "Already caught that one. Maybe I'll go back for seconds."

Sam shuddered as the image of his aunt and their neighbor filled his mind. "Anyway, moving along here. I'm happy in Hobson Hills, and Teague lives across the country."

"Sam," Mia said softly. "I see the way you light up when you talk to him. If Dougal, or whatever the man's name is, is out of the way, what's holding you back? The truth this time."

He stomped his foot. "You and Teague always think you know everything. Fine, Aunt Mia. I refuse to lose Teague. I *will not* fall in love with him and chase him off, especially since Teague is a five hundred on a scale of one to ten for best-friend quality. Even distance doesn't stop us from being there for each other, and I'm not going to fuck that up."

"You didn't used to be such a coward," Mia said, scowling. "It's time you get over that ex of yours and take what's standing right in front of you. Well, right there on your computer screen every night."

"I *am* over Brett, Aunt Mia. That doesn't mean I'm going to risk my friendship with Teague, just because I get lonely at night." Sam gave her a stubborn look. "I'm going to date every damn alpha in Hobson Hills and be happy about it."

Sam ignored Mia's laughter and stalked out the door.

He stood on the porch and tried to clear his head. His aunt lived in a large ranch-style home on the edge of Hobson Hills. Years ago, a dairy farm had owned all the open pasture and wooded area behind the house, but the owners had moved away from Maine a long time ago. Sam had always loved the peaceful place.

No noisy neighbors or heavy traffic, and all the fresh air I'll ever need. The clear summer day was warm, but not yet hot, and Sam could hear Gramps Wilson's tractor as he mowed hay in the pasture across the road.

It pulled him straight back to his childhood. After his mom had died, his dad couldn't handle his grief, let alone raise an eight-year-old. He'd sent Sam to Mia, then lost himself in a bottle.

Life with Mia had been wonderful, and Sam really did love the woman, even if she was annoying sometimes.

He shook himself and headed for his car. If he couldn't get some peace in his own home, he would go to work early and start planning how he'd demolish his aunt's ugly kitchen.

"I *won't* fall in love with Teague," he muttered, pushing all thoughts of the sharp-chinned alpha from his mind.

CHAPTER 4

eague paced around his office. "Puff, we have a problem."

His bearded dragon looked up from where he sat on the windowsill, basking in the sun. Today was Puff's day to accompany Teague and Tortellini to work.

"He's dating..." Teague's hands curled into fists. "...for real this time."

Puff blinked lazily and laid his head back down.

"It is too a problem," Teague argued. "I know alphas, and they'll be all too eager to take advantage of Sammie while he's vulnerable."

Puff's eyes narrowed.

"Okay, so Sam's an adult and can take care of himself, but that doesn't mean that I don't have a responsibility to be there for him. I'm his best friend, damn it." Teague ran his hands through his hair, absently noting it was time for another haircut. "There's only one thing to do."

He stalked back to his desk and picked up his phone. Sam would be at work right now. Teague dialed Aunt Mia's number.

"Hey, handsome," she answered, her smile carrying over in her voice. "Are you ready to run off to Vegas with me?"

Teague grinned. "Don't tease me, you flirt. I'd be there in a heartbeat if I thought you were serious."

She chuckled. "How are you doing, Tee?"

"Horrible." Teague plopped down in his office chair. "I miss Sam, Mia. I know he belongs in Hobson Hills with you, but he's my best friend. How am I supposed to be there for him if I'm all the way across the country? He told me he was dating now too. What the hell am I supposed to do from Seattle?"

"Oh, I know." She hummed. "There's all these alphas hanging around now. You know Maine grows 'em big. They eye my Sammie like he's a plate of bacon."

Teague growled. "Sam is more than just a tasty omega. He deserves someone who appreciates and loves him, not some… some buff lumberjack who just wants a piece of ass."

"You got that right." She sighed. "I worry about my tater tot. He's a sweet boy, but I'm just one person, and I'm in no shape to protect him all by myself."

Teague took a deep breath. "I think I need to move to Hobson Hills. That's the easiest solution, right? If I'm right there with Sam, we'll have a better chance of surviving a zombie apocalypse."

"A zombie what?" Mia snorted a laugh. "Excuse me, I mean to say that's the best idea. You should definitely move here, because of the lumberjacks and the zombie apocalypse."

"I checked for animal sanctuaries and there wasn't one listed near Hobson Hills." Teague rubbed his chin. "I have the money for the land saved, and I bet there are pets needing rescued right now. They *need* me to be there."

"Well, we have Doc Grover, and… you know what? You're exactly correct. There are probably a ton of animals needing you. Let me get Gramps Wilson's number for you. That man knows everything going on in town. I'll talk with our local veterinarian too. He's a good man who could use some help."

"Thanks, Aunt Mia." He wrote down the number she gave him. For the first time in over a year, Teague felt like he had a plan, and the damn worry and stress he'd been carrying around was slowly disappearing. "I've had a few people interested in my clinic, so I'll start closing things out here. Will you keep an eye on Sam until I can get there?"

"You bet, handsome." Mia sounded happy.

"You'll take care of yourself too, right? Sam said you were overdoing it during the day while he was gone."

"Oh, you boys. I'll be fine. Someone's always checking in on me while Sam's gone anyhow. My friend Barbara is even coming by later to watch our shows."

"Okay." Teague hesitated. "It's just that we love you, and we want you to be around for a good long while."

Mia sighed. "I can't wait to meet you, Teague. You're getting a great big hug from me."

After the call ended, Teague called and left a message for Gramps Wilson, then got back to work.

"You look happy, Doc," Katie said, smiling at him as she weighed their next patient, an Australian Shepherd named Gomer. "Dare I say, there's a bounce in your step?"

Teague fought back a smile. "There's nothing better in life than having a solid plan."

LATER THAT EVENING, he replied back to the e-mail from another veterinarian in the area that had expressed interest in buying Teague's clinic. The man worked in a larger clinic and was ready for his own place.

"Never thought I'd sell my place, Orville." Teague rubbed his pig's chin, smiling when Orville grunted happily. "You'll like it in Maine, buddy. I'll get a place with a big yard, so you can do some more running."

"Meow." Noodle eyed him from her perch in his lap.

"You, Noodle princess, will never have to worry about a backyard. I know your paws are too dainty for the outdoors."

Morris cawed softly from his perch by the window. The African Grey parrot had spent a great deal of the year moping. Teague hadn't told Sam, but he was worried about Morris's health. The bird loved Sam and lived for their video chats.

"Just another reason to make this move." Teague took a moment to pet Morris and feed him a bit of greens. "We'll both be happy to have Sam near us again."

His cell rang and he answered it without checking the number. "Hello?"

"Teague Walsh? This is Gramps Wilson from Hobson Hills."

Teague's brows raised. It was late in Maine, so he was surprised at the call. "Thanks for calling, sir. Mia Baldwin said you might know about some land for sale. I want to open an animal rescue sanctuary."

"I happened to talk to Mia today, and I know just the place for you. I'll send you the info in the morning. Our local veterinarian is interested in talking to you too." Gramps cleared his throat. "I'm glad Sam will have a friend in town. He's a good kid, but a bit shy. Taking care of Mia has kept him busy this year, but we've been trying to get him out of the house a bit. I think my grandson Abel is arranging a date for Sam for the weekend. It's with a young alpha friend of his. A lumberjack, I think. Abel says he's a good-looking fella with plenty of muscles. I hear some omegas like that kind of thing."

Teague scowled and poked his own soft belly. He had some muscles of his own, but he probably needed to hit the gym more often. "Fucking lumberjacks. How soon can you get that information to me? I have a buyer interested in my veterinarian clinic."

"I'll send it now," Gramps said smugly.

After the call ended, Teague grabbed his laptop and called Sam. "Damn lumberjacks are a menace," he grumbled, pulling Luna, one of his three black cats, onto his lap. Luna was a good snuggler.

A few minutes later, Sam connected to the call. "Hey, you're calling early."

"Took a half day today." Teague soaked in the sight of Sam's smiling face. He liked seeing Sam happy, even if it was on a screen. "How was the date last night?"

Sam groaned. "You'll never believe what happened with Adam."

"Tell me." Teague fought back a smile. He shouldn't be so happy that Sam obviously didn't have a good time.

"We met at the diner in town, and I thought it was going really well." Sam scrunched his nose. "That ended when we left. We passed Caden—he's a nice alpha who's married to the bookstore owner—and Adam gave him this disgusted look, then said that a grown man shouldn't carry a rabbit strapped to his chest. Huckleberry is a good bunny and Caden's best friend. Why wouldn't he carry Huck with him when he goes somewhere?"

Teague grinned. "It makes perfect sense if they're best friends."

Sam nodded. "Exactly. So that was the end of Adam. I don't need any more assholes in my life, thank you very much."

"Good," Teague said smugly. "You can't trust lumberjacks."

Sam tilted his head. "Huh? Are lumberjacks still a thing? I mean, they must exist, right? We have lumber."

Teague waved his hand. "Forget lumberjacks. I need to introduce you to Mimi."

Sam gave him an exasperated look. "Another pet?"

"I found her in the dumpster behind the clinic." Teague bent and picked up the kitten. "Isn't she the sweetest kitten you've ever seen? She loves Tortellini, so really, she's his kitten, not mine."

"Oh, that makes it okay then." Sam laughed. "She is adorable."

CHAPTER 5

*S*am parked his car in front of Zoe's bakery. He didn't have to be at work for another hour. "Cinnamon-roll break."

His phone rang before he opened the door, and he sighed when he saw the screen. "Hi, Brett."

"Hey, babe." Brett had that slight whine in his voice that he got when he was annoyed. "Can you email Martin your recipe for lasagna? His tastes like shit, and we're having my boss over for dinner tomorrow night."

"I didn't think Martin liked cooking," Sam said, frowning. He didn't want to share his recipes with the *other* omega, damn it.

"He doesn't, but my boss expects a homecooked meal, so someone has to make it."

Sam rolled his eyes. *How about you cook, asshole?* "Okay, I'll send it to him."

"Thank you," Brett said, satisfied. "I don't know what I'd do without you."

Brett hung up before Sam could reply.

"I really need to block his number." Sam sighed and looked around. "Shit, now I'm talking to myself."

He got out and waved to Caden and his husband Yeo. The two had their children with them and were leaving the diner.

Small town life wasn't perfect, but there were a few things Sam really liked. Knowing almost everyone in town was one of them.

A familiar blue truck parked next to him, and Gramps Wilson got out.

He smiled at Sam. "How you doing, Sammie?"

"I'm about to get one of Zoe's cinnamon rolls, so I'm really good."

"Let me get it for you," Gramps said. "You and I need to catch up anyway."

"You don't need to do that." Sam held the door open for Gramps.

"It's my pleasure, kid. Go grab us a seat." Gramps grinned and nudged him toward the booths. "Go on."

Sam shrugged and picked out a booth. He watched Gramps laugh and chat with his granddaughter, Zoe, before carrying a tray to their table.

"Zoe said you'd want a latte too." Gramps passed him the cup and then slid one of the plates to him. "There's your cinnamon roll. Now, tell me how Mia is doing. She never tells us the truth."

Sam snorted. "Don't I know it. She's doing pretty well, all things considered. She still wears out easily and takes a lot of naps. Her appetite is a lot better since she's not doing the treatments anymore, so that helps."

"I noticed she'd put on some weight when I saw her yesterday," Gramps said, nodding. "Laurel and I thought she looked a lot better."

"Her hair is growing back faster than we expected too."

Sam sipped his latte. "I didn't realize how happy that would make her. To me, it's just hair, you know?"

"A lot of people are attached to it," Gramps said, tugging on his own white beard. "In more ways than one."

Sam rolled his eyes and laughed. "You're ridiculous."

"Seriously, though, she's really doing okay?" Gramps asked, eyes worried.

Sam smiled softly. "She really is."

"How about you?" Gramps asked, smiling mischievously. "You've been dating a lot, I hear."

"I'm just fine." Sam hummed happily as he bit into his cinnamon roll.

"*Fine*," Gramps repeated, making a face. "When people say they're fine, they usually don't mean it."

Sam pointed his fork at Gramps. "Why does everyone want me to bare my soul?"

Gramps grinned. "Just keeping you honest, kid."

Sam huffed. "So, I'm not completely fine. I'm happy about staying in Hobson Hills, but I miss my best friend from Seattle."

Gramps rubbed his chin. "Tell me about him."

"His name is Teague, and he has a thousand rescue pets. He's a veterinarian, and he *may* have a mushier heart than Doc Grover."

Gramps gasped, clutching his hand to his heart. "Is that possible?"

"It is." Sam leaned forward to whisper. "His dream is to open an animal rescue sanctuary. He's going to take in *so many* pets. He'll have his own pack of dogs soon."

Gramps laughed. "You like him a lot."

"I do." Sam propped his chin on his fist. "He has an African Grey parrot named Morris who's my one true love. He tells me I'm beautiful and can sing 'I Will Always Love You.'"

"You miss both of them." Gramps gave him a sad look. "Do you need to talk to Doc Grover about getting a pet of your own?"

"I can't cheat on Morris." Sam sniffed. "I don't roll like that."

Gramps snorted. "My mistake."

Sam sighed. "For real though, I don't want to leave them behind, but I love it here in Hobson Hills, and Aunt Mia still needs me, even if she won't admit it."

His phone chimed with a text, and he looked at it before rolling his eyes and stuffing it in his pocket.

"That couldn't be Teague," Gramps said. "You wouldn't look that annoyed with him."

"My ex wants me to send one of my recipes to his new omega *right now*." Sam pressed his lips into a hard line. "Like I have nothing better to do. I don't even know what's he's doing up right now. He should be sleeping instead of texting me."

Gramps scowled. "He shouldn't be texting you at all. That man has some nerve. He's lucky he's in Seattle or my Laurel would be bailing Mia and me out of jail."

Sam chuckled. "Aunt Mia has made it her personal hobby to think of ways for Brett to die. It can't be healthy, but it sure is fun."

"Do you miss that one?" Gramps asked, arching a brow. "You were awful taken with him."

Sam bit his lip. "Sometimes I think I do. I like being someone's person."

"Did you like being *Brett's* person?"

"That's the real question." Sam drank the rest of his latte. "It's too pretty of a day to talk about Brett. Tell me how the Wilson clan is doing?"

Gramps snorted. "You have to work today, don't you? I don't think there's time for that."

LATER THAT DAY, Sam hummed under his breath and swayed to the song stuck in his head as he sliced carrots for the next batch of steak and ale pies. He enjoyed cooking and working behind the scenes at The Irish Rose. He stayed busy assisting the cooks on duty and helping with the catering jobs.

Brett had always thought Sam should have gone to culinary school, but that hadn't been something Sam was interested in. He loved cooking, but he didn't love it *that* much. Sam just liked feeding people and making them happy. His job at The Irish Rose let him do that, and his bosses, Justin and Abel, were wonderful.

Reuben, the morning cook at the pub, worked on the other side of the kitchen, his big body moving with perfect efficiency as he prepared a rack of chicken and vegetable pasties. The quiet man was a steady and calm presence. He didn't like to talk much, but he was always kind, and listened to Sam when he had issues to talk through.

Justin pushed open the door of the kitchen, arms full of dirty dishes. He gave Sam a wink and stacked the dishes at the sink.

"I'll get those in a minute, Justin. I just need to finish the prep." Sam often doubled as the dishwasher in the morning too.

"No problem. We have plenty of clean plates and silverware." Justin washed his hands, then bumped Sam with his shoulder. "I got an alpha for you."

Sam sighed. He should be happy, but honestly, he could use a little break from dating. "What's his name?"

"Wow, you sound like I'm about to send you to take out the garbage," Justin said, laughing.

Sam chuckled. "I can't help it. I've been on so many dates,

and none have worked out. Either it turns out there's no chemistry, or the man is an alphahole."

"Ah, the agony of dating," Justin said, wincing. "Your man is out there somewhere. We'll keep trying."

What if I already met my man? he thought. *What if he wanted someone else?*

"By the way, that minced beef wellington of yours was a hit." Justin smiled wide. "We are officially making Wednesday nights, Sam's Beef Wellington nights."

"Told you," Rueben said.

"I should have listened." Justin headed for the door. "Feel free to offer more suggestions, Sam. You're a good cook, and we know it."

Sam hid his smile. It felt good to know people liked his food.

"Brett wasn't it." Reuben's deep voice startled Sam.

"Huh?" Sam asked, puzzled.

"Brett wasn't your person." Reuben gave him a look. His friend knew all about Brett since *that* day—the day Brett and Martin got married, and Sam had broken down in tears while trying to work. He had hated that it had upset him so much, that Brett still had a hold on him, but he had loved the alpha for years.

"I loved him," Sam whispered, turning back toward his vegetables.

"Did he love you?" Reuben leaned against Sam's table.

"I think so..." Sam frowned. "Maybe."

"Doesn't matter." Reuben shrugged one large shoulder. "We don't just get one chance at love."

"This is the most you've ever spoken at once," Sam teased. "What are you trying to say?"

"Relationships take work." Reuben crossed his arms. "Sometimes they last. Sometimes they don't. Love isn't a fairy-tale fix-it-all."

Sam gave him a disbelieving look. "I've seen you and your husband. Ernie adores you, and the two of you together are my couple goals. Seriously."

Reuben grinned. "I love Ernie, but it still takes work from both of us."

"I put in the work with Brett." Sam huffed. "You see how well *that* turned out."

Reuben slowly moved back to his own station. "Yeah, but one day, you'll find the person that will put in the work for you."

CHAPTER 6

Teague closed his office door and braced his forehead against the cool wood. *Signing paperwork sucks*.

He pushed back and looked around the bare room. The only items left were business purchases, so he didn't feel right taking them with him.

The door slammed open, and Katie rushed inside. "Did you do it?"

Teague nodded. "Vintman agreed to keep the current employees after he takes over the clinic. You and the others won't lose your jobs."

Katie let out a relieved breath. "Thanks, Dr. Walsh. We're going to miss you around here."

He patted her arm. "I built a great team here, and Vintman appreciates it. The clinic won't even close during the transition. You all are going to be fine."

She gave him a grateful smile. "I can't believe you're doing this."

Teague shrugged. "It feels right."

Katie gave him a doubtful look. "If you say so."

His phone chimed, and he took it from his back pocket to check the time. "I need to meet Dad for lunch. I'll see you when I get back."

"Have you, uh, told him yet?"

He winced. "I'm going to do it at the restaurant. That way he won't make a scene."

Katie snickered. "Good luck with that."

Teague left the clinic and walked a block to the small bistro his dad loved. He had to admit he'd miss Seattle, but there was no doubt in Teague's mind that he needed to do this.

His dad was waiting for him at his favorite table. Timothy Harrington was a lovely omega in his early sixties. His professionally styled hair fit well with the tailored slacks he wore. Anyone looking at him probably wouldn't believe that Timothy had spent most of his life as a single father working two jobs. The omega had taken care of them after splitting with Teague's deadbeat alpha father.

"Hey, Dad." Teague kissed his dad's cheek before taking the seat across from him. "Thanks for meeting with me. I know you and Dennis are only in town for a few days."

Timothy waved his concern away. "I love seeing you. Dennis will be joining us soon too. He had a phone call to take."

Teague nodded, pleased. "It'll be good to see him again, but can you please try to talk to him about his *donations*. He keeps putting money in my account, then tells me he owes me for sending you on that cruise five years ago."

Timothy patted his hair and fluttered his eyes. "He met me on that cruise, son, and you know I'm the best thing that's ever happened to him. He's just thankful."

Teague fought back a smirk. "I still don't want his money."

"Dennis wishes his own kids felt that way. The two youngest keep arguing about increasing their trust funds."

Timothy eyed him. "You look nervous. What's going on? Please, don't tell me you're finally upset about breaking up with Dorian. If you actually feel relief after a breakup, then it needed to happen."

"I'm still okay with Dorian being gone." Teague fought back a yawn. Packing up his office and house was exhausting, especially when his menagerie kept getting in the way.

Timothy propped his chin on his fist. "Is it about Sam? I know you miss him. I really need to meet him."

Teague's cheeks flushed with heat. "I'm moving to Hobson Hills, Maine."

Timothy gave him a blank look. "You're moving where?"

"A small town in central Maine."

"Where the ticks are?" Timothy narrowed his eyes. "I don't think all those animals of yours will like getting ticks."

Teague snorted. "Ticks don't solely exist in Maine."

His dad rolled his eyes. "What about your animal rescue sanctuary? You were looking at that place near Leavenworth."

"Gramps Wilson found me some property in Maine." Teague scanned the menu, already knowing what he'd order. "It was cheaper and more land than I expected. He also talked the local veterinarian into hiring me part-time."

"Gramps Wilson?" Timothy gave him a baffled look. "His name is Gramps? What the hell is going on?"

"Sam," Teague said simply.

Understanding softened Timothy's eyes. "Ahh, I see."

"He's staying in Hobson Hills with his aunt."

"How is she doing?" Timothy asked.

Teague tapped his menu on the table. "Really good, but she needs him nearby, and he wants to stay close to her."

"I don't blame him. Family is important." Timothy grabbed Teague's hand and squeezed it. "So, you're moving to Hobson Hills to be with Sam. Did you tell him you love him?"

Teague pulled back and gave his dad a confused look. "What are you talking about?"

Timothy gave him a flat look. "You're telling me that you're selling the business you built from the ground up, moving across the country with all your pets, and opening an animal sanctuary in a small town in Maine just to be close to your *best friend?*"

"That's what friends do, Dad." Teague set his menu down. "I need my best friend to be happy, and Sam needs to stay in Hobson Hills. It makes perfect sense."

"How did I raise an idiot?" Timothy asked the ceiling of the restaurant. "I thought I did well by him, Lord, but where did I go wrong?"

"What's wrong, pookie bear?" Dennis asked as he sat in the chair next to Timothy. Teague's stepdad was shorter than Timothy and had a little bit of a belly. His steel-gray hair was styled, and he wore a suit that looked more expensive than Teague's car.

"My son doesn't know he's in love with Sam." Timothy sighed dramatically and leaned his head on Dennis's shoulder. "Tell me he's still maturing and will eventually grow some sense."

"He turned thirty-six last month," Dennis said, grinning at Teague. "Sam is that omega you talk about all the time, right?"

Teague nodded. "He's my best friend. I'm just moving to be closer to him. If the zombie apocalypse happens, we need to be close to one another. There's nothing strange about that."

Timothy moaned. "It's hopeless. He's even buying land from someone named Gramps Wilson."

Dennis chuckled. "For your sanctuary? Did your dad tell

you I have some other sponsors for you? He won't be the only one donating this year."

"He didn't, but that's great. I appreciate you asking around. Schmoozing isn't my thing, but the sanctuary will take a lot of money to run."

Dennis nodded. "It's a good cause, and the least I can do for family."

Teague tapped the table nervously. "It's hard to believe it's finally happening. I've been saving money for years, and this place is perfect. Gramps sent me pictures, and it has three barns, a full stable, and is fenced in. I'll be set up to take in rescued farm animals too. There's no house on it, but it's right behind Sam's aunt's place, so I figure I'll stay with Sam and Aunt Mia until I build a house."

"I'm happy for you." Dennis wrapped an arm around Timothy's shoulders. "Maybe if you spend more time with Sam, you'll finally realize you're in love with him."

Teague groaned. "I'm not—"

Timothy interrupted him with a gasp. "You're right, love muffin. This really is perfect." He patted Dennis's chest. "We spend all that time in New York too, so we'll be able to visit more often. I'll finally be able to meet this best friend of yours."

"When are you leaving?" Dennis asked. "I'll make sure to have the jet available for you."

Teague flushed. "I can't ask you to do that. I don't mind driving there."

Dennis waved his hand. "Nonsense. You never let me help you with anything, and you have all your pets to think about. You'll take the jet and hire a driver for your things. I insist."

Teague wanted to argue, but Puff in particular wouldn't do well with a long road trip. "I won't argue. It really will be a lot easier."

"You just want to see Sam quicker," Timothy said, giving

him a concerned look. "Are you sure about this, Teague? I'm forcing myself to ignore your zombie apocalypse comment, but it's concerning me."

Teague took a drink of his water and tried to find the right words. "I can't imagine not seeing Sam every day. This year has been hard with the distance between us. We've been there for each other, but there were so many times I just wanted to hug him, Dad. Brett the Bastard broke his heart, and he struggled so much taking care of his aunt. He's too stubborn to take care of himself. He needs me."

Timothy gave him a sad look. "That poor boy. I understand, sweetie."

Teague leaned back and crossed his arms. "Plus, he's started dating again. He's not ready for that, Dad. There's probably a hundred buff lumberjack alphas ready to take advantage of him. I need to watch out for him."

Timothy's eyes went wide, and he slowly turned his head to stare at Dennis. "Did he really just say that?"

Dennis winced. "He's your son when he says stupid things like that, pookie bear."

"What's stupid about wanting to be there for your friend?" Teague said, scowling. He hadn't been able to sleep a full night all month as visions of dancing lumberjacks filled his dreams.

"You're hopeless." Timothy rolled his shoulders. "Alright. Dennis and I will find as many sponsors as we can for your sanctuary. You focus on *protecting* Sam and investing in tick treatment."

LATER THAT NIGHT, Teague held Niles, his hairless Sphynx cat, up in front of the laptop screen. "See, he likes the sweater you sent him."

Sam laughed, dark eyes dancing with humor. "My friend Ernie made it for him. I told him how many pets you had, and he's working on matching sweaters for everyone, you included."

Teague gave Niles a doubtful look. The cat looked good in his knitted pink turtleneck, but Teague didn't think *he* would.

"That's a lot of sweaters." Teague shrugged. "I'm not gonna think about it."

"You have five dogs, six cats, two hamsters, five birds, a bearded dragon, a miniature pig, and a tortoise." Sam gave him a hard look. "You need those numbers, Tee."

"Lalala." Teague held Niles up to his face. "Don't tell me the numbers. Just say *that's a lot of sweaters to knit.*"

Sam grinned. "It won't stop him. Ernie recruited both the knitting *and* quilting clubs."

Teague had to fight a smile at how happy Sam looked. His friend enjoyed life in Hobson Hills. He couldn't wait to surprise him next week. Mia had already given him permission to stay with them for a little bit, so Teague had held off on telling Sam of his plans.

His burgeoning smile turned into a frown. "How was the date tonight?"

Sam groaned. "It was horrible. Kent reminded me of Brett—overbearing and obnoxious."

Teague grinned. *You said it, not me,* he thought to himself. Brett was a self-centered piece of shit.

"Brett called yesterday, you know." Sam tapped his chin. "He spent the whole call ranting about traffic, which is just plain annoying. He didn't even ask about Aunt Mia. I think he was just bored on his commute home so he called me."

"Why is he still calling you?" Teague didn't like the thought of Brett wiggling his way back into Sam's life.

"He says we're still friends," Sam said, rolling his eyes.

"I take it you're not seeing this Kent guy again?" Teague asked, ignoring the sourness churning in his gut at the thought of Sam dating anyone. *It's just that no one can possibly be good enough for my best friend. That's all.*

"Nope," Sam said, lips popping on the *p*. "Now, let me talk to Morris. After that horrible date, I need to see my one true love."

CHAPTER 7

A week later, Sam danced in place as he sliced potatoes to stock up for The Irish Rose's famous pub fries. It was Friday afternoon and the lunch rush was only now slowing. Sam knew the evening cook would need more if the tourist crowds kept coming.

Reuben looked a little frazzled, but he got that way during the summer tourist season. "You're staying late?" he asked.

"Yeah." Sam grinned over his shoulder. "Albie won't have to face the crowds alone tonight."

"Justin and Abel need to hire more help," Gramps said. "You boys can only handle so much."

Members of Reuben's family usually visited during lunch hours, and Gramps Wilson currently sat at the break table eating his favorite, a plate full of Irish boxties and chicken pasties. Reuben's husband was a Wilson, so Gramps was a frequent visitor.

Reuben shrugged. "They're interviewing."

"I hope they're not teenagers." Sam groaned. "We serve alcohol, so it won't be teenagers, right?"

Reuben chuckled and shook his head.

"Teenagers aren't so bad. Oh, hey, Sam. I meant to tell you." Gramps's voice was full of mischief. "The Thompsons sold that property around your house."

Sam spun around, mouth falling open. "They did? I thought they wanted to keep it in the family."

Gramps shrugged. "None of the younger generation seemed to want it, so Chuck decided to sell out."

"You bought it, right?" Sam turned back to his potatoes. "Justin told me you were wanting it for your son's cattle."

"Well," Gramps said, drawing the word out. "I was going to, but I got a call from a man that was looking for land in Hobson Hills, and the Thompsons' place was perfect for him."

Reuben grunted, and Sam gave him a look. His friend looked amused.

"What's so funny?" Sam asked them, baffled. People called Gramps all the time when they needed something. The older man had his hand in everything in Hobson Hills.

Gramps chuckled. "Nothing you need to worry about. I think your new neighbor is coming by for lunch. You'll figure it out then. Say, did Justin tell you about my buddy's grandson? His name is Judd and he's an alpha. Justin was supposed to set you up for Saturday night."

Sam sighed. He had dated what seemed like every single alpha in the county, and was no closer to finding his special someone. "Yeah. We're going to the movies."

"Not happy?" Reuben asked, voice low and gravelly.

Sam thought about it a moment. "I don't know. Maybe I'm being too picky."

"Nope," Gramps said, voice firm. "Settling for someone won't make you happy. Take the time to find the person you want."

"Brett?" Reuben asked Sam, arching a brow.

"I don't know," he finally said. "He called yesterday and asked me to housesit for him and Martin when they go on vacation in October. I told him I couldn't fly out there just for that, and he actually asked where I was."

Reuben's eyes narrowed and he scowled.

Gramps's expression went hard. "That man needs to leave you alone."

Sam's shoulders slumped. "I really need to stop answering his calls. After I told him I was still in Hobson Hills, he still wanted me to housesit."

Reuben grunted again and gave Sam a hard look.

"No, I didn't agree to do it," Sam said, fighting back a smile. "Teague would have killed me."

Gramps grinned and that mischievousness was back. "I really do like Teague."

"He's been my BFF for years now, so you know he's the greatest." Sam starting swaying again as he sang to himself. *This song won't get out of my head.*

"Poor Judd," Gramps said, laughing. "Maybe Abel knows another omega that wants a date."

Sam looked over his shoulder. "Huh?"

Before Gramps could answer, the door to the front opened, and Justin stepped inside. Sam liked Justin, he really did, but he wasn't sure about the look in Justin's eyes. The other omega appeared way too excited.

Justin grinned at Sam. "Oh, my sweet little Sam. You've been hiding things from me."

Sam's eyes widened. "Okay, so I ate the pot pie that was supposed to go to Doc Grover. It had onion in it, and he doesn't like onion. I just didn't want it to go to waste."

"What?" Justin frowned, then rolled his eyes. "No, no, no. I mean you never told me about the hot alpha that's asking to see you."

"What hot alpha?" Sam asked. An image of Brett's face

filled his mind for a moment, and he was surprised at the lack of interest he felt. *Teague*, however, would definitely be a hot alpha.

Justin smiled sweetly and fluttered his eyes before opening the door. "Why don't you go see?"

Sam frowned and set his knife down before washing and drying his hands. "I'll be right back, Reuben."

Gramps chuckled. "Take your time. I'll wash up and chop those potatoes."

Sam gave him a curious look, then nudged Justin with his elbow. "Why is everyone acting so strange?"

Justin didn't answer him as he shoved Sam out the door.

Sam stumbled over his own feet, but fortunately stayed upright. He looked around, noting the familiar faces. North carried a tray of food to one of the tables. Mateo passed out cold mugs of beer at the bar and took lunch orders. Teague stood with Doc Grover at the door.

Wait.

Teague stood with Doc Grover?

Sam's brain froze for a second, and a loud squeal filled the pub. He barely recognized it as coming from him as he flew around the bar and into Teague's arms.

"You're here? Oh my god, you're really here!" Sam wrapped his arms around Teague's waist and hugged him tight. He buried his face against his friend's chest and savored the familiar scent. "I missed you so much."

Sam felt the tightness in his shoulders and neck start to slowly loosen. He'd been carrying a weight around since the day Aunt Mia called and told him about the cancer. *Teague's here now. Everything will be okay.*

Teague squeezed him close and lifted him off his feet. "Missed you too, Sammie."

He had needed a Teague hug more than he realized.

~

SAM STARED at Teague in shock. "You're moving to Hobson Hills?"

Teague shook his head. "I've *moved* to Hobson Hills. Me and all my babies are staying at your place until I either find a house or build one. Aunt Mia gave me permission."

Sam pinched his arm. *Yep, that hurt. This must be real.* That was really Teague sitting across from him. They sat at a table on the patio. Justin had insisted Sam take a break and visit with his friend, which Sam had appreciated. He was too excited to see Teague to focus on work anyway.

Teague looked good, his brown hair mussed by the wind. Most importantly, there was no regret hidden in his warm eyes. He just looked happy to see Sam.

"What about your clinic? Did you hire a manager?" Sam asked.

"Sold it." Teague picked up the menu and started looking over it. "What's good here?"

"Everything," Sam answered, then smacked the menu down. "You sold your clinic? That was your pride and joy."

Teague shrugged. "It was time for a change, and you want to live in Hobson Hills. No big deal."

Sam leaned back and eyed his friend. "Are you having a mid-life crisis?"

"I'm not feeling the need for a fast sports car, if that's what you're asking," Teague said with a smirk.

Sam snorted. "Okay. I'm not going to question this anymore. I'm just going to enjoy having you here. Now, order the pub fries and Rueben's Fritters. Then I'm introducing you to everyone."

Teague gave him one of his rare smiles. "I finally met Aunt Mia in person. I think I'm in love."

Sam picked up his own menu and smacked Teague on the

head. "Don't even think about it. She's way out of your league."

The next hour passed fast as they talked about Teague's animal rescue sanctuary and Sam's ideas for remodeling the house. They even outlined a plan of action in case of a zombie apocalypse.

Before Sam knew it, he had to get back to work.

He hugged Teague again, reluctant to let him go. "You promise you're not a figment of my imagination? You'll be home when I get there?"

Teague hugged him back. "I'll be there. So will Morris and all the others. Oh, and Doc Grover gave me another pot-bellied pig. His name is Wilbur and he's kind of big. His previous owners overfed him, then sent him to Grover when he wasn't a cute little piglet anymore."

Sam looked up, worried. "Maybe you shouldn't work for Doc. Maybe you shouldn't be allowed to talk to the man. He has a habit of foisting pets off on unsuspecting people."

"Are you kidding me? He's a great guy." Teague squeezed him again. "You may have competition for the title of my best friend."

Sam gasped dramatically and looked around. "Where's Grover? I'm kicking his ass."

AFTER HIS SHIFT, Sam hurried home. Teague had texted him pictures of the pets settling in with Aunt Mia all afternoon, and it had taken everything in him to not leave work early.

He parked under the carport and watched two of Teague's dogs chase Nugget around the front yard. Orville, and who could only be Wilbur, ran with them, grunting happily.

Poor chubby boy, Sam thought, giving Wilbur a soft look.

Teague's new pig was black and white like Orville, but Wilbur was almost twice the other pig's size.

Sam left the car and opened the front gate, laughing when the herd descended on him.

"Hi, Lily." He scratched behind the fluffy brown dog's ears. "You're looking good, little lady. Oh, and look at you, Percy."

The gray pit bull was next, and Sam bent down to let the sweet dog give him some kisses. Percy's back legs were paralyzed after he had been hit by a car as a stray. Someone had found him and brought him to Teague. Now, he had a doggy wheelchair for his back legs and moved around well.

"You've grown since I saw you last, sweet boy." Sam gave him one more kiss on his head, then laughed when Nugget pushed in beside him.

Today, Nugget was wearing a panda hat. Sam could see the golden retriever's shortened tail now and wanted to cry at what the poor pup had been through. "Nice to meet you, Nugget. Thank you for your kisses. Yes, I really needed my ear licked."

Orville ran to him, squealing softly. Wilbur followed slowly behind, a little unsure.

Sam hugged Orville and scratched the miniature's sides. "Missed you too, Orville."

Wilbur stepped closer, and Sam stayed still, letting the new pig come to him to investigate. Honestly, Sam was surprised at how well Wilbur was doing with the other animals already. After a moment, Wilbur seemed satisfied that Sam wasn't there to cause trouble, and ran off with the rest of the animals. This time, they all chased Lily.

Sam laughed and watched them play for a few more minutes before noticing Noodle watching him from the window. He bowed low in her direction, and she turned around, stretching her body out before settling down for a nap.

Sam rolled his eyes and went inside. Normally, the house was pretty quiet, but Sam could hear Morris's chatter from the door, and the latest pop song played from a Bluetooth speaker next to a large birdcage in front of the living room windows. Teague's three parakeets, Triton, Ariel, and Seagra, warbled along to the tune.

The shrill sound of a telephone went off in the room and he looked up. Binks was perched atop the bookcase. The Cockatiel tilted his head and shrilled again, sounding almost exactly like an old landline phone.

Sam chuckled, then looked down when movement caught his eye. Two hamsters rolled past him in their balls, and Tortellini, Teague's tortoise, slowly crawled after them, a small, fluffy gray and white kitten sitting on his back. Sam hadn't met Mimi yet, since the kitten was one of Teague's newer additions, but she looked like she was having way too much fun riding Tortellini.

"Teague's cooking dinner," Mia said, drawing his attention.

His aunt sat in her favorite chair, an old, beige recliner. Teague's oldest dog, Merle, sat in her lap. The small Maltese was blind and didn't usually take to new people quickly, but Merle seemed perfectly content with Mia. Two black cats, Luna and Dove, stretched along the back of the chair and watched him with golden eyes.

Sam crossed his arms and tried to ignore how cute his aunt looked surrounded by pets. "You knew Teague was moving here and you didn't tell me."

Mia gave him a smug look. "What's your point?"

He stomped his foot, almost stepping on Charlie's tail as the three-legged black cat wound between his feet. Sam bent and picked Charlie up, feeling bad. "I would have been better prepared. I looked like an idiot today, squealing at the top of my lungs and wrapping myself around him."

Mia chuckled and looked around. "That sounds like a *you* problem, sweet potato. Now, I may have underestimated the sheer number of pets your man has."

"I told you about all of them," he said, giving her a look. "It's too late now. You'll just have to love them all."

Moose decided that was the perfect time to come greet him. The Great Pyrenees ran in from the kitchen and jumped, knocking Sam and Charlie to the floor.

Sam giggled as Moose licked his face. "Stop it, Moose. Bad boy."

Moose stopped licking his face and looked down at him with sad eyes.

Sam set Charlie down and hugged Moose's head. "I can't stay mad at you. You're a good boy, I swear."

"Don't lie to him." Teague's grinning face appeared above him, Binks now perched on his head. "Welcome home."

Sam's breath caught in his chest, and he didn't think it was *just* because Moose lay on him. *Damn, when did Teague's smile get that sexy?*

"My love. My love. My one true love."

Sam squealed and sat up quickly, startling Moose. "Morris!"

Morris flew from the kitchen and landed on Sam's outstretched arm. "Here I am, beautiful."

Sam gently rubbed his head and back. "I missed you so much, Morris."

"Missed you." Morris dipped his head shyly. "Beautiful."

Mia snorted a laugh. "Here all your friends were trying to find you a boyfriend. Looks like you already have one."

Teague chuckled. "Morris loves Sam."

Sam bent and kissed the parrot's head. "I love Morris too."

CHAPTER 8

Teague waited for Sam on the couch. He already had most of the pets settled down for the night. A renovation show was pulled up on the television, and a bowl of popcorn sat ready and waiting. He hadn't been this happy in a year.

Back in Seattle, he and Sam had spent a lot of evenings together with the pets and the television. Teague's job left him exhausted at the end of the day, and Sam had been on the outs with Brett more often than not.

Dogs, cats, and pigs were strewn about the room, all resting after a very eventful day. Charlie and Niles shared his lap, and Nugget sat beside him on the couch.

He faintly heard Sam shut the door to Mia's room down the hall, and a moment later, his friend was settling himself on the other side of the couch. Mimi and Lily immediately took over Sam's lap.

"She doing okay?" Teague asked, nodding down the hall.

Sam smiled, eyes happy, but exhausted. "Yeah. It's just been a big day, and she gets tired easily."

"Will the pets and I be too much for her?" Teague hated

the thought of leaving, but he knew that he'd effectively taken over Mia's home. Hell, her sunroom had become Morris and Binks's territory. Then there was the sheer number of them. They weren't exactly inconspicuous.

Sam shook his head. "She loves you all already. Merle, Luna, and Dove belong to her now. They're sleeping with her tonight."

Teague looked around. "I wondered where they were. It's okay. I have plenty to spare, and I know where Mia lives."

Sam scratched Lily's ears and leaned his head against the back of the couch, dark eyes focused on Teague. "We're both happy you're here, but are you sure about this, Teague? Hobson Hills is a lot different than Seattle."

Teague shrugged. "You're here."

Sam rolled his eyes. "You make no sense, but it doesn't matter. You've had a chance to run. Now, Aunt Mia is attached to you all, so you have to stay."

"You just want my help with the renovations." Teague nodded toward the television. "I already have ideas."

Sam smiled. "I don't just want you here for free manual labor."

Teague fluttered his eyes. "Aww, really?"

"I also missed Morris."

"Wow." Teague leaned back into the couch. "The pain is unbearable."

Sam's laughter made something light up in Teague. His friend had been having such a hard time of it lately, and Teague liked seeing happiness on his face.

Sam reached across the back of the couch and punched Teague's shoulder. "I think you'll live."

They settled in to watch the show, but Teague was more focused on Sam. Having Sam beside him felt right in a way nothing else had in a very long time. *Has he always had those dimples?*

Teague shook himself. His dad's words were just getting to him. Sam was just his friend.

THE NEXT DAY, Sam led him down Main Street, Percy's leash in one hand and Nugget's in the other. "Here's the diner, The Cozy Kitchen. Gib owns it and makes the best omelets you'll ever taste. Then there's Zoe's bakery, Honey Buns. She orders in that fancy coffee that you like so well and makes cinnamon rolls that I would sell my firstborn for."

"Hmm, but would you sell Morris?" Teague asked, biting back a smile. He braced his hold on Lily's leash when she tried to push ahead. The small dog was hard to walk. Moose, however, plodded along at the perfect speed, tongue hanging out.

"Never." Sam's nose went in the air. "You aren't supposed to trade your one true love for a cinnamon roll. Friends, on the other hand, are fair game."

Teague laughed. "I feel loved."

Sam bumped him with his shoulder and nodded toward the next shop. "That's the Book Worm. I need to go in and get the latest Roxanne Baxter release."

"You and your romance books." Teague noted the *Pets Allowed* sign and looked down.

Puff's head poked out of the top of Teague's button-up shirt. The bearded dragon was in his walking harness, but he preferred riding to walking. He was also a little shy around new pets.

Sam held the bookstore's door open, and Teague went in. He breathed a sigh of relief when he saw there weren't a lot of people inside. The only pet was a rabbit playing in a child's playpen near the cash register.

Teague looked down again.

Puff looked up at him, then back at the room.

"We'll just be here for a minute," Teague whispered.

"It's okay, Puff." Sam smiled at the bearded dragon. "You'll like it here when you get used to everyone."

A very pregnant man stepped out from the shelves and smiled at him. "Sam! I have your book ready. Signed and everything."

"Thanks, Yeo." Sam smiled. "This is my friend, Teague. He just moved here from Seattle."

"I take it all of these are yours?" Yeo said, smiling at the dogs. "Mia avoided getting another pet after Sparkles died, and I know Sam was reluctant to have one since he was in love with a bird or something like that."

Teague grinned at Sam. "You've been pining for Morris? Why didn't you tell me? I would have brought him to you."

Sam flushed. "With Aunt Mia's treatments, I didn't have time to give him the attention he needed."

"Can I pet them?" Yeo asked, shuffling his feet. "I really need to pet them."

Teague nodded. "They're friendly."

They chatted for several minutes before Yeo was finished playing with the dogs. "I almost forgot," the man said and waggled his eyebrows at Sam. "I know this really nice alpha and got his number for you. His name is Saul, and he's friends with the Wilsons. You want to meet him Friday night?"

Teague couldn't read the expression on Sam's face, but he recognized the sourness twisting his stomach. He *really* didn't want Sam to date anyone, but he didn't want to admit why. Every time his friend told him about a date, he should have been happy for him. Instead, he practically danced with joy when they inevitably went bad.

"He's busy." The words came out before Teague could

stop himself. He ignored Sam's shocked look. "That's when we're going to the movies. Remember?"

"No," Sam said, drawing the word out and giving him a suspicious look.

Yeo blinked, looking a little uncertain. "Oh, well, I know a nice omega too. His name is Griff, and I'm sure he'd like to meet you, Teague. It could be a double date."

"No," Sam said loudly, startling the dogs.

Teague arched a brow and watched his friend dance from foot to foot.

"We don't have time for a date that night. We're giving Morris and Binks baths. Remember?" Sam asked, giving him a hard look.

Teague frowned. Binks took baths in his water bowl every morning, and Teague knew Morris showered with Sam. It was kind of weird, but he'd helped Sam install a little bar in the corner of the shower just for the parrot.

"Oh," Yeo said, looking between them. "Well, you could always go out with them next weekend."

"Teague doesn't like dating," Sam said, voice getting high as his eyes darted around the room. "He's… um… it's against his religion."

Yeo tilted his head and gave Teague a questioning look. "Really?"

Teague shrugged. "Sure?"

He didn't understand why he liked the fact that Sam didn't seem to want him to date anyone. He really liked a possessive Sam.

"I guess I'll just give Saul your number then, Sam?" Yeo asked, a smile tugging at the corner of his mouth.

"Absolutely not." Teague scowled at Yeo. "We don't even know this Saul guy. Plus, Sam doesn't want to date anymore. He needs to…" Teague thought for a moment. "He needs to figure himself out."

Sam gave him a dry look. "Seriously? That's the best you can come up with?"

Teague arched a brow. "It's the truth. Trust me. Lying is also against my religion."

Yeo drew their attention. The pregnant man's shoulders shook with his laughter. "Gramps was so right. You two have it bad for one another."

Teague shook his head. "What are you talking about?"

Yeo tried to stifle his chuckles. "Gramps and a bunch of others saw you all at the pub. He said it was obvious you two were really into each other. Why try to hide it?"

Sam's cheeks flushed an intriguing shade of red. "We're just friends. I'll come back for the book, okay? We have a thing to get to."

Sam headed for the door, but Teague's feet seemed frozen to the floor. *Is Dad right? Am I in love in Sam? I'm old enough that I should know my own heart by now, right?*

"Teague?" Sam tugged on his arm. "Come on. Let's go home."

"Home," Teague whispered, closing his eyes. When had Sam become home? They'd been apart for a year, and while Teague knew he had missed Sam, he was starting to realize he hadn't known how *much* he'd missed Sam.

"Are you okay?" Yeo asked softly, eyes kind. "I didn't mean to upset you two."

Teague cleared his throat. "I'm okay. Sorry about that. Let me get Sam's book for him."

Sam bent and petted Nugget and Percy. He gave Teague a concerned look. "I know we're just friends, Teague. I won't get ideas. Okay?"

Teague shook his head. "What are you talking about?"

Sam looked away. "I just mean that you don't have to worry about me making things weird."

"I'll just ring his book up." Yeo smiled nervously and hurried to the register.

Teague ignored the man, attention focused on Sam. "How would you make things weird?"

Sam gave him a frustrated look. "Are you really going to make me say it?"

"I'm so confused." Teague groaned. "I shouldn't have said you didn't want that guy's number. I just want you to myself. I missed you."

He ignored the little voice in his head telling him that he was full of shit. *I definitely am not sabotaging Sam's dating life because I'm in love with him.*

Sam gave him a considering look. "Yeah. *That's* why I told Yeo you didn't want to date. We just need some us time. Once people get used to seeing us together, they'll realize we're not like that."

"You're right." Teague cleared his throat. "It's not like anyone would *really* believe you and I are a couple anyway. Not if they really knew us."

Sam's laugh sounded off. "Seriously. We would make a horrible couple."

Horribly wonderful. "Definitely," Teague said, trying not to sound depressed.

Sam turned toward the register. "So, you and I will take some friend time. I really like that idea. Of course, I have a date tonight that I already set up, but after this one, I'll let everyone know to hold the setups."

Teague narrowed his eyes and followed Sam. "Tonight? Give me details."

The burning hot rage flaring through Teague at the thought of Sam going out with someone, now that Teague was there, told him that *maybe* he *was* as full of shit as his dad thought.

Sam had a hard time focusing on the movie. It was a recent release that he had been eager to see, but this date was just so awkward.

He smiled at Judd. The alpha seemed nice enough and was good-looking with dark skin and beautiful brown eyes. His smile was wide and kind. Most importantly, he didn't seem to mind that Teague sat on Sam's other side, which said a lot about the man's good nature.

"Popcorn?" Judd whispered, angling the popcorn bag toward Sam.

"He prefers M&Ms mixed in," Teague whispered back, before shoving his own popcorn bag at Sam.

Sam sighed. "I'm fine, Judd. Thanks."

"No problem." Judd bit back a smile and handed Sam a pack of gummi worms. "I got the gummies you wanted."

Sam took them. "Thank –"

"He likes gummi *bears*," Teague said, and tossed a box of gummies on Sam's lap. "You don't know anything about Sam."

Judd nodded, face solemn. "You're right. Sam and I should

spend some time together to get to know one another. You know. Maybe go on a date."

Sam snorted and almost choked on his mouthful of popcorn.

Teague glared at the other alpha. "Very funny. All you lumberjacks are alike. You just want in Sam's pants."

Sam tilted his head. "I didn't know you were a lumberjack, Judd."

Judd arched a brow. "Neither did I."

The woman in front of them turned around and glared at Sam and the two alphas. "Be quiet! We want to watch the movie, not listen to your drama."

Sam blinked innocently and got another handful of popcorn and M&Ms.

"Sorry," Teague and Judd both muttered.

The rest of the movie was uneventful, and it wasn't long until the lights were back on and Sam was on his feet, gathering his things. He still had half a bag of gummi worms, but had eaten all of Teague's popcorn and candy.

"That was good," Judd said, smiling at Sam. "You have good taste in movies."

Teague snorted. "His favorite movie is *Attack of the Killer Tomatoes*. Trust me. His taste in movies isn't that good."

Sam smiled at Judd as he elbowed Teague in the gut. "Do you want to grab a drink at The Irish Rose?"

"Normally, I would say yes." Judd gave him a wry look. "I kinda think you're taken, whether you realize it or not."

Sam's cheeks flushed, and he stuffed a gummi worm in his mouth. "Teague and I are just friends."

"Obviously, you're intimidated by our close bond, so off you go." Teague shooed Judd toward the exit. "Nice to meet you and all. Don't expect Sam's call."

Judd shook his head and laughed as he left the theater.

Sam turned around and smacked Teague's arm. "What the

hell, Teague? You show up at the theater and then go out of your way to be an asshole to Judd. He seemed like a nice-enough guy."

Teague gave the exit a dark look. "You don't know what kind of man he is."

Sam rolled his eyes. "Neither do you. That's the point of dating someone. You learn about them."

"We're taking friend time. Remember?" Teague linked his arm in Sam's, and they left the theater. "Do you really want to go to the pub? I could use a beer after that horrible date."

Sam growled and stomped on Teague's foot. "You're obnoxious. We're going home, and you're going to tell me what the hell is wrong with you."

"Ouch." Teague danced on one foot for a moment before glaring at Sam. "There's nothing wrong with me."

Sam sighed. He knew why *he* would be upset if Teague was going on a date with some omega. What he didn't know was what was going on in Teague's head.

"Teague, do you really not want me to date?"

They came to a stop at the car. Teague leaned back against it and crossed his arms. "We've never been single at the same time before. Not since we met."

Sam felt his phone buzz and looked down. He recognized Brett's number.

"That's Brett, isn't it?" Teague shoved off the car and unlocked the doors. "Go ahead and answer it."

Sam grabbed Teague's arm. "No. You're more important than him. Tell me what's wrong."

Teague turned around. "Am I? You love him, don't you? What if that's him begging you to come back?"

Sam started to shrug off Teague's questions, but the look Teague gave him made Sam stop and think. Teague was upset, and he *never* got upset outside of the veterinary surgery room.

Sam thought about Brett. He had invested years in their relationship. He had loved the alpha. He *had* loved the alpha. *Past tense.*

"I don't love him anymore," Sam said quietly, shock filling him. "I think, for a while, I was stuck in the pattern of letting him use me. He calls, and I answer. He asks for a favor, and I do what I can."

Teague's brown eyes were dark with emotion. "Do you want him back?"

"No." Sam smiled and shook his head. "Even as lonely as I am, if he were calling me to get back together, I'd tell him to shove his head up his ass."

Teague swallowed hard. "Good. That's good."

Sam moved closer and slid under Teague's arm to hug him. "You should know that you're far more important than anyone in my life, except maybe Aunt Mia."

Teague hugged him and balanced his chin on top of Sam's head. "You're important to me too. I can't imagine life without you in it."

"Maybe." Sam paused and took a breath. He couldn't believe he was about to say this. "Maybe you're more to me than you should be. We *haven't* been single at the same time before, but that doesn't mean I haven't thought about what we could be like together."

Teague's arms tightened around him. "You've thought of us together? Like sex?"

Sam squeezed his eyes shut, cheeks heating. "Not just sex. I've thought of us together as a couple."

Teague was silent for a long moment. *Good job losing your best friend, dumbass,* Sam thought, fighting tears. *He just got here, damn it.*

He finally managed to look up, eyes widening at the smile that covered Teague's face. His friend looked like Sam had just handed him the moon.

Teague cupped Sam's face and watched him with wonder. "I've wanted you for a long time, Sam. When we met, you were with Brett, so I made myself give up the idea of us together. I never could forget though. I hated him so much for not treating you like the dream you are."

Sam smiled slowly. "Teague, do you want to go get a beer?"

Teague gave him a suspicious look. "Are you trying to get me drunk so you can have your way with me?"

Sam shook his head. "Nope. I want to get you drunk so I can steal your herd."

"They're already yours. So am I," Teague said, eyes soft.

Sam's laugh cut off when Teague pressed his lips to Sam's. Heat coursed through him as his tongue explored Teague's mouth. The man's taste was addictive, and Sam knew he'd spend as much time as possible kissing Teague.

Sam groaned when Teague's arms tightened around him. Teague pushed him back against the car, hands on Sam's hips. When Teague lifted him, Sam wrapped his legs around Teague's hips and deepened the kiss.

Teague's warm hands ran up the sides of Sam's thighs, and Sam shuddered, dick hardening quickly. He moved his hips against Teague, feeling the alpha's erection pressing against his own.

A bright light shining in Sam's eyes made him pull back, breaking the kiss. The headlights of a truck lit up the darkness around them.

Judd's head poked out the window. The man grinned at them. "I'd suggest getting a room, guys. Congrats on figuring things out.

Sam hissed and made a face at the man. "Go away. I finally have Tee exactly where I want him."

Teague buried his face against Sam's shoulder and shook with laughter. "You heard him, lumberjack. Go away."

Judd chuckled and drove away.

"So, how about that drink?" Sam asked, joy filling him at Teague's smile.

"Sounds like a good first date," Teague said and kissed him again.

Teague's gonna be mine now, Sam thought happily, wrapping his arms around Teague's neck. *All mine.*

CHAPTER 10

Teague flipped a pancake, then settled it on the small stack in front of Sam. "What time do you work this morning?"

Sam fed a piece of broccoli to Morris and smiled. "Ten to six, so you're on your own with cleaning out that barn."

Teague groaned. "Why do you need to work? You should stay here and help me for free."

Sam shook his fist in the air. "Damn bills and their need to be paid."

Mia chuckled and sipped her coffee. "You just don't want to shovel old shit, sweet pea."

"That *may* be a very small part of it," Sam said, grinning. He buried his pancakes in syrup and took a big bite.

Teague put another pancake on Mia's plate.

She arched a brow, but took a bite. "So, are you two gonna explain the silly grins you keep sneaking each other? Is this a best friend thing?"

Sam patted his mouth with his napkin and gave her a prim look. "Aunt Mia, I thought you were aware of this, but when two people really like each other—"

"Did you two finally pull your heads out of your asses?" Mia interrupted, grinning.

Teague sat down with his own plate of pancakes. "Our heads are very much out of our asses, thank you."

"Thank goodness." Mia whooped loudly, startling Morris, and the other pets gathered around the table in the hopes of someone dropping some food. "I knew getting you two in the same town again would do it. Gramps owes me a hundred bucks. He said it would take at least a month."

Sam snorted. "I should be upset that you're betting on my love life, Aunt Mia, but I'm too happy." He gave Teague a heated look. "I have plans for you."

Teague cleared his throat and shifted in his chair, his pants suddenly much tighter. "Good to know."

Mia snickered and took another bite. "You two better keep the fucking to your rooms. I've seen Sam's ass plenty enough. Just last week, he was running through the hall naked."

Teague arched a brow and looked at Sam. "Oh, really?"

"No lumberjacks were involved," Sam said, rolling his eyes. "I ran out of clean towels."

By the time breakfast was finished, Teague had come to terms with shoveling shit by himself. Sam and he washed dishes, while Mia played with Merle, Dove, and Luna.

"She loves those three," Sam whispered. "I'm glad I waited on getting her a new pet."

"Me too." Teague sighed. "I miss cuddling with Luna, but Aunt Mia needs her more."

Sam bumped him with his hip. "I'll cuddle with you."

"Meh." Teague shrugged. "I guess that will do."

Sam snapped a dish towel at him. "You love my cuddles and you know it."

Teague laughed and handed Sam a plate. "You're alright."

"Go clean out your barn," Sam said, pointing at the door. "By yourself."

Teague looked around at the dogs and pigs sprawled around the kitchen. "I can't at least take one?"

Sam sighed. "Okay, one."

After a long debate, Percy was the only one that seemed remotely interested in leaving Sam. Teague watched him carefully as they walked along the gravel path leading to the barn. Percy's back wheels seemed to handle it alright, but the dog was used to sidewalks.

"I'll get this paved for you, Perce." Teague scratched behind his dog's ear and surveyed the land he had just bought.

The acreage was mostly pasture, but had some wooded area toward the northern end. A gravel drive led from the road to the main barn, but that was it. Gramps had told him that the place had been used for hay for years now, so the barns and stable weren't in the best shape, though they were still usable.

His phone vibrated in his pocket, so he took it out and glanced at the screen before answering. "Hey, Dad."

"Teague?" Timothy sounded shocked. "Why do you sound happy? Are you smiling? You sound like you're smiling."

"Sam and I are dating," Teague said smugly. "All the damn lumberjacks in the world can go fuck themselves."

"Already?" Timothy laughed. "Didn't you just get there a couple of days ago?"

"Don't judge me." Teague sniffed. "Anyway, this is a great place, Dad. There's a ton of space, and I really like the local veterinarian. He has a lot of connections in the area and is going to help me get the word out there once I open."

"Yes, yes, rescuing animals is important. Tell me about you and Sam. Is it serious? When did it happen?" Timothy sighed happily. "This is the one for you. I know it. You never sound this happy when you start dating someone."

"It's Sam," Teague said simply. To him, that made all the difference in the world. "Are you sure that I really need to have a grand opening for the sanctuary? I know Dennis said you two were gathering sponsors for me, but will they actually want to come to Maine just for an opening? As many of my exes have pointed out, not everyone loves animals as much as I do."

"They really will, son. Most of Dennis's friends like to donate to good causes, but many of them actually like to *see* those causes." Timothy chuckled. "Dennis is really playing you up to them too. He admires you a lot and his friends can tell. Of course, his kids aren't too thrilled about that."

Teague rolled his eyes. "They aren't thrilled about anything to do with me."

Dennis's first marriage had ended in divorce, and his three children hadn't been happy when he'd remarried. They especially didn't like that Teague got along so well with Dennis.

"Audrey and Henry are mad that he's donating to your sanctuary," Timothy said dryly. "They seem to think he should increase their trust funds instead. Sterling, of course, thinks I'm stealing all of Dennis's money and laundering it through you."

Teague scowled. "You aren't like that."

"I know, sweetie." Timothy sighed. "I won't lie. I like that Dennis has money, and I like spending it. That's not why I married him though. I never thought I'd marry anyone after your father left us. I didn't think I could trust an alpha again."

"That's why I get mad when those three get snobby." Teague knelt down and hugged Percy. "They see you and Dennis together, so they should be able to see how happy you make each other."

"Hmm, you mean how I noticed you and Sam belonged together?" Timothy sounded amused. "Yet, somehow, you didn't realize it."

"Okay, so maybe people can be oblivious." Teague smiled at Percy. "I wish I had said something to Sam sooner."

"Things happen when they're supposed to happen," Timothy said.

Teague groaned. "I hate it when you say stuff like that. I like having control of my own life."

"How about this," Timothy said wryly, "Sam wasn't ready for a relationship with you until now. He wouldn't have cheated on Brett, you know that, and you said that he's only now starting to date."

"*Me*," Teague interjected. "He's starting to date me. I'll take care of him and make sure he knows how amazing he is."

Timothy laughed. "You have it bad."

"I really do." Teague sighed. "I can't fuck this up, Dad. Sam is my best friend, and if I mess up, I'll lose him all together."

Timothy was quiet for a moment. "Let's say that Sam suddenly developed an allergy to all pet fur and he couldn't take medication. What would you do?"

Teague held his phone away from him and gaped in horror. He finally put it back to his ear. "Why would you even say something like that?"

"Just answer the question," Timothy said, laughing.

"We'd still be able to keep Puff, Tortellini, and Niles around us, but I guess I'd have to buy a second home for the others." Teague hugged Percy again. "I could set up a decontamination room in the utility room and split my mornings."

Timothy's laugh boomed through the phone. "That's your answer, Teague. Your first thought is to work something out, not to leave. You won't fuck things up more than we all do occasionally."

"I can't even deal with you right now." Teague shuddered.

"Why would you even put that thought out in the universe like that? I'm hanging up, and I'll be waiting for your apology." He hung up as his dad continued to laugh. "Percy, what the hell is wrong with him?"

"Woof." Percy grinned, tongue hanging out, and ran ahead of him.

Teague shook his head and tried to enjoy the nice September day around him. Fall hadn't quite arrived yet, but a cold front would be moving through next week. Sam was looking forward to the leaves changing and the cooler temperatures. His omega even liked snow.

Teague shuddered again. He froze when he saw a black truck parked in front of the largest barn. A trailer was attached to the back and piles of rotted wood already filled it.

"Percy, is someone stealing our rotted wood?" he whispered. "If so, we should just leave them to it."

The barn doors were open, and Gramps Wilson and an unfamiliar young man came through, each carrying an armful of wood.

Gramps tossed the load of wood into the trailer, then waved at him. "Hey, Teague. I thought you'd like some help getting things cleaned up here."

"Seriously?" Teague's eyes widened. *Is this man for real?*

Gramps gave him a sharp look. "I've known Mia my whole life. She adores Sam, and we're pretty fond of him too."

Teague cleared his throat, suddenly feeling very vulnerable. "You've heard already, haven't you?"

Gramps chuckled. "The whole town has. You two will be good for one another. Now, do you want our help?"

Teague nodded, smiling wryly. "I'll take any help I can get. It's been a while since I've done anything harder than lifting a Newfie to the exam table."

"I'm glad I brought one of my grandsons then." Gramps

patted the young man on the shoulder. "This is Tomás. He's one of my youngest's sons."

Tomás smiled shyly and knelt down to pet Percy. "The barns are all in pretty good shape. We'll need to replace some of the boards and give it a coat of paint, but most of the work is inside. Have you thought about what kind of layout you want?"

Teague pulled his notebook from his back pocket. "I've been planning this my whole life. I have all kinds of ideas."

LATER THAT NIGHT, after Mia and the pets were asleep, Sam straddled Teague on the living room couch as they kissed. His omega's lips were highly addictive, and Teague knew, no matter what happened between the two of them, he would always crave Sam.

"Teague." Sam moaned against his mouth and lifted his hips. Teague couldn't stop himself from rocking against him, relishing the feel of Sam's hard dick pressing through his pants.

He reached between them and unbuttoned his pants, freeing his erection. He rolled Sam's sweatpants down his hips, then wrapped his fingers around his and Sam's dicks, stroking them. Teague's other hand gripped Sam's ass, keeping him pressed tightly to him.

"You feel so damn good," Sam said, breathless. "Why didn't we do this the day we met?"

"Fuck if I know." Teague moaned and bit down on Sam's lip. His grip on Sam's ass tightened, and he pulled him closer, their dicks rubbing hard against one another in fast motions.

Teague felt it coming. Everything inside him pulled tight, but he needed something to push him over the edge. Sam's shudders as he came did it.

Sam's smaller body pulled tight, and he groaned as he came, splattering against Teague's stomach and dick, fierce satisfaction filling his dark eyes.

Damn, he's beautiful, Teague thought, coming hard at the feel of Sam's hot cum on his skin. He kept his arms wrapped around Sam, enjoying the feeling of his weight against him.

The faint light from the television played across Sam's skin, and his warm breath puffed against Teague's neck. *Fucking perfect.*

Sam took the last plate from the dishwasher and dried it off before stacking it with the others. His hips shifted side to side as he sang along to the tune playing through his earbuds. He still had a few hours left of his shift, but he couldn't wait to get home to Teague.

The past month had been one of the best of his life. He was in the town he loved and had a man that treated him like he was a flawless fucking diamond. *Teague is mine, all mine.*

Sam knew he should probably be a little more concerned about how fast they were moving, but it felt like they were making up for years of just being friends.

A finger poked him in the side, making him jump and squeal in a very manly fashion.

Justin stood beside him, grinning. "Your man is having a late lunch with Doc Grover. I thought you might want to take your break."

Sam tried to look casual. "Yeah, sure. I guess that will work."

He ignored Reuben's deep chuckles and removed his apron and washed his hands.

Justin smirked at him as he walked past him. "No humping your man in the pub."

Sam stuck his nose in the air. "I make no promises."

Once he was free of the kitchen, he gave up any pretenses and hurriedly dodged customers and servers until he was at Teague and Doc's table.

Teague grinned and pushed his chair back so Sam could sit on his lap. "Taking your break?"

Sam buried his face against Teague's neck and breathed in his scent. "Uh huh. You all are a little later than usual. Busy day?"

Doc Grover groaned. "Let's just say, it's a good thing I hired Teague to help out."

"We have our first rescue." Teague gave him a nervous smile. "Zoe Bethel found a stray nosing around the dumpster behind the bakery. It's a little Pomeranian mix. The poor little guy's malnourished and has bald spots all over."

Sam frowned. "It's early October. The poor baby was living outside?"

Teague gave him a soft look. "Why did I even doubt it?"

Sam tilted his head. "Huh? Doubt what?"

"Journey's going to be dog number six." Teague shook his head. "You don't even care, do you?"

Sam shook his head baffled. "Care about what? Journey clearly needs to be taken care of, and that's kind of the whole purpose of having an animal sanctuary. I know you're not technically open yet, but that shouldn't matter. A dog with bald spots will be hard for Doc Grover to adopt out. People can be shallow."

Teague hugged him tight. "I love you."

Doc Grover choked on his drink, and water dripped from his mouth.

Sam couldn't bring himself to ask if Doc was okay. All he could do was stare at Teague's wide smile. "You love me?"

"So damn much." Teague huffed out a laugh. "I don't even care that we've not been dating long. I know you. I trust you. I love your heart. You're kind, funny, fucking adorable. I can't help it."

"You're definitely all mine now." Sam cackled. "Mine, mine, mine. I'll never let you leave the house, and you have to help me pick out new flooring for the kitchen. I get to keep all the pets too. This is the best."

Teague arched a brow. "Care to tell me anything in return?"

Sam gave him an innocent look. "I'll still let you play with the pets."

Teague groaned and tightened his arms around him. "Sam."

"Okay, okay." Sam laughed. "I love you too, Tee. I've loved you forever. I just didn't realize it until we kissed. Don't tell Aunt Mia. I think her and Gramps have a bet going about when we admit we love each other."

"Too late." Doc Grover cleared his throat and patted his face with his napkin. "I already texted them. Damn Gramps won. I had six months on. Mia was betting on next month."

Sam couldn't smoosh the happiness bubbling inside him enough to care. "You love me."

Teague pressed his forehead to Sam's. "I love you."

A sudden thought had Sam scowling. "Damn it, now I have to go back to work with a hard-on."

Teague pressed his own erection against Sam's hip. "You aren't the only one."

Doc Grover waved a hand in the air. "Justin, bring the spray bottle. They're talking about hard-ons."

SAM HURRIED to his car after work. He couldn't wait to get

home to tell Aunt Mia that Teague loved him. He strapped his seatbelt and pulled out.

I'm making chicken parm tonight, he thought. That was Teague's favorite, and Sam had some chicken in the refrigerator.

His phone rang through his car's Bluetooth and saw it was Brett. "Ugh, not today Satan." A few moments later, the phone rang again as Brett called a second time. "Sure, I have nothing better to do than talk to you." Sam sighed and answered the call. "Brett."

"Martin's sleeping with our neighbor." Brett sounded like he was discussing his dry cleaning instead of his husband's infidelity.

"Mr. Rawlings?" Sam made a face. The older man was nice, but he didn't understand the concept of bathing.

"No, Rawlings moved out two months ago," Brett said sharply. "I'm done with Martin."

"Wow." Sam blew out a breath and turned his blinker on at the stop sign. "I'm sorry, Brett. Have you talked to Martin? Maybe you two can work it out."

"I don't think you understand," Brett said slowly. "Martin's gone. I want you back."

Sam laughed, hard. *What the actual fuck?*

He turned onto the highway and started toward home. "Brett—"

Sam didn't see the truck pull out, but he felt the impact to the passenger side of his car. His air bags burst out and his head slammed back against the seat. Black dots danced in front of him, and his vision blurred before he passed out.

SAM WOKE up when the paramedics pulled him out of the car. He yelled as they pressed his leg into something.

"Shit, sorry," one of them said. He couldn't tell which one since he was seeing double.

"It's going to be okay, Sam." Sam recognized the voice. It was Tanner, Justin's husband.

"Are you arresting me?" he asked, his words slurring, and his vision dimmed again.

When he woke again, he was in a hospital bed. His body hurt all over, and his leg was in a cast and propped up on a pillow.

"Sammie?" Teague's face came into view. "Shit, you scared us."

"What happened?" His voice was scratchy and his throat dry.

"Hey, tater tot." Mia appeared at his other side. "The youngest Erickson boy missed a stop sign and hit you."

"Damn it." He could feel sleep pulling at him. "Am I okay?"

"Concussion, two broken ribs, lots of bruising, and a broken leg," Teague said, voice hard. "That asshole should be sitting in a jail cell."

"It was an accident," Mia said, running a hand over Sam's. "You're going to be okay, baby boy."

"The nurse said he was awake?" A man poked his head in the door and smiled at Sam before slipping into the room. "I'm Dr. Norwell. You've been in and out of consciousness for a few hours now. We want you to get as much rest as possible tonight, and we'll reevaluate in the morning."

"I'm sleepy." Sam blinked at him. "It hurts."

"I need to speak to you alone before we give you more pain meds," Dr. Norwell said.

"Why?" Teague asked, eyeing the doctor.

Mia tugged on his alpha's arm. "We'll be right outside. Come on, caveman. Dr. Norwell isn't going to attack him."

The doctor waited until Teague and Mia were outside

and the door was closed before looking back at Sam. "I won't keep you from your sleep long, I promise. When we bring patients in like this, we always run a lot of tests to determine if there are any underlying concerns we need to be aware of."

Sam made a strangled sound. *Cancer. They found cancer.*

The doctor gave him a small smile. "We discovered that you're pregnant, Mr. Baldwin."

Sam's mouth fell open and relief filled him. "Pregnant?"

"It's very early on, less than a month." The doctor patted his hand. "We're keeping this in mind with everything we're prescribing you."

"Thanks." Sam's words came out as a squeak.

"I'll let you get some rest, young man." The doctor left the room, and Teague and Mia came back in.

"What's wrong?" Teague asked, giving him a concerned look. "You're paler than when we left you."

"Nothing," Sam managed to say. "Nothing's wrong."

"Oh, good." Mia pressed her hand to her chest. "Gramps is here to give me a ride home. I'll see you in the morning, peanut. I love you."

"Love you too." He watched her leave. "Is she okay?"

"Gramps and his wife are going to stay with her tonight to watch the pets and make sure she gets some rest." Teague sat at the edge of the bed. "You scared us."

"Sorry." Sam reached for Teague's hand and squeezed it. "I didn't even see him."

"Your Bluetooth was on." Teague looked away. "Brett called. He wanted to know what happened, so I told him. He said that he would book a flight for you back to Seattle after you're recovered."

Sam closed his eyes. "I hurt too much to laugh at that. I remember now. Right before the accident, Brett told me he wanted to get back together."

"What did you say?" Teague's voice was soft.

Sam opened his eyes and gave his alpha a disbelieving look. "Did I not just tell you that I love you, Tee? Was that today or have I been unconscious for years?"

"You loved Brett a long time." Teague finally looked at him, and Sam wanted to cry at the pain he saw in his man's eyes. "I just want you to be happy, Sammie."

"I want to be happy too." Sam reached for the cup of ice, and Teague handed it to him. "I deserve to be happy, and you know what makes me happy?"

"What?" Teague helped him tilt the cup.

Sam chewed on the ice, the cold easing his dry throat. "You. You make me happy. Now shut the fuck up and get in bed with me."

Teague's laugh was short and wet. "Are you sure?"

"One hundred percent." Sam closed his eyes. "I love you."

CHAPTER 12

A week later, Teague propped his head on his fist and watched Sam sleeping beside him, Noodle curled against head. It hadn't taken long for them to start sharing a bed since they were already sharing a house.

Now their lives were so emmeshed that Teague couldn't imagine Sam *not* being at his side. Everything felt right, as if Sam had been the missing piece to the puzzle of Teague's life this whole time.

He heard stirring and looked farther down. Dogs, cats, and two pigs were spread across the massive, custom-made bed. Niles watched him from where he slept between Charlie and Lily. The Sphynx wore red flannel pajamas and a peaceful expression.

Wilbur snuffled in his sleep and rolled to his side, trapping Sam's good leg beneath him.

Sam startled awake, shaking his head and interrupting Noodle's beauty sleep. The Siamese gave them both a dirty look and stretched slowly.

Sam rubbed his eyes and yawned. "What time is it?"

"Almost time to get up." Teague leaned over and kissed

him. "I'm going to feed the herd. I'll be right back. Don't move."

Sam gave him a heated look and snuggled under the thick blanket. "If you insist."

Teague's dick told him to hurry the hell up, so he quickly slid out of bed, dodging Nugget and Mimi. As soon as his feet hit the floor, every animal in the room was awake and ready to eat.

Five dogs, four cats, and two pigs followed him down the hallway to the kitchen, eager for their breakfast.

Mia was already awake, and it looked like she had fed Merle, Dove, and Luna. She sipped her coffee and watched him fill food and water bowls. It took some time since each animal had their own nutritional needs or medications.

"Good morning, beautiful." Teague gave Mia a kiss on the cheek and refilled her coffee cup. He led Wilbur into the laundry room before giving the big guy his breakfast. Wilbur had a habit of finishing his own meal quickly and stealing the other pets' food, so he had to eat alone.

Mia chuckled and gave him a considering look. "I just now figured out why Sam's damn bird is so charming. Morris has been around you too much."

Teague preened at her praise. "I'm a good role model."

Mia rolled her eyes and slowly stood. "I feel like making waffles. You boys have thirty minutes to fool around before breakfast." She shooed him toward the doorway. "I'll let the critters out after they finish eating."

He kissed her cheek again. "You're the best, Aunt Mia."

She laughed when he bolted back down the hallway, hurrying to the bedroom.

Sam gave him a sleepy look before sitting up. "That was fast."

Teague didn't bother explaining. He slid onto the bed and

rolled into Sam, careful of his broken leg, his body pressing his omega down into the mattress.

Sam hooked an arm around his neck. "I love you."

Teague hummed in pleasure and gently nipped Sam's neck. "I love you too, Sammie."

He took a moment to admire how lovely Sam was in the gray morning light filtering through the large window. His omega's dark hair was mussed and his cheeks covered in morning scruff.

Sam's eyes went from sleepy to heated in a flash, and he pulled Teague down for a kiss. "I had a little fun while you were feeding the herd."

Teague arched a brow and pulled the covers down Sam's body. His omega was completely bare beneath, his good leg cocked to the side. Teague could barely see the end of Sam's favorite butt plug.

"Sammie." Teague could hear the raw need in his voice. "You're my favorite person."

Sam stroked his dick, then ran one hand to his hole. "You noticed this, huh?"

Teague moved to kneel between his legs. "I'm observant like that. You're ready, aren't you?"

Sam tugged on the end of the plug and groaned, spreading his legs wider. "So damn ready."

"Fuck, so am I." Teague pushed his pajama pants down and stroked his own hard dick as he watched Sam pull the plug out, then push it back in.

Teague took over and spent a few moments fucking Sam with his plug. Sam moaned, head thrown back, and pumped his dick faster. "I want you in me, Tee."

"I'm good with that." Teague slowly removed the plug and pushed a finger into Sam's tight hole.

Sam groaned. "More."

Teague obeyed and added a second finger. He groaned too when Sam began fucking himself on Teague's fingers.

"Enough." Teague's body shook as he pulled his fingers free from Sam's lubed, stretched ass. "I want to come inside you."

Sam nodded, eyes watching Teague's hand on his dick. He pulled Teague close, and the alpha settled between Sam's legs.

Teague gripped his omega's hips, rubbing his dick over Sam's stretched hole. He leaned down and pressed his mouth against Sam's, losing all ability to think. His tongue wrapped around Sam's, and he drank up his contented sigh.

Teague stroked Sam's dick once, using his thumb to rub at the pre-cum leaking from the head.

Sam's moan was hungry, and Teague positioned his dick and slowly pushed inside Sam's tight ass. Teague's grip on Sam's hips tightened, and he pushed until his balls rested against Sam's ass.

He cupped the back of Sam's neck and kissed him as he set a fast rhythm, riding his omega hard. Teague got lost in sensation, the taste of Sam on his tongue, and the feel of his omega's body around his own, driving him.

It wasn't long before Sam came, groaning deeply as he shuddered below Teague.

Teague grasped Sam's hips and moved faster, pounding into him. When he was close, he bit down into Sam's shoulder, making him shudder with pleasure as Teague came deep inside him.

Teague held Sam close for several moments as their breathing calmed. He tightened his arms around Sam and kissed the top of his head.

"Teague." Sam pulled him into another kiss, and Teague went willingly, his omega's taste heating him from the inside out.

Knocking on the door made them pull apart. "You two

better be getting dressed," Mia yelled. "Breakfast is almost ready, and you still need to feed the rest of your menagerie."

"Yes, ma'am," Teague called out, stifling his laughter.

Sam chuckled against his chest. "She has a point, you know. We have a big day ahead of us."

Teague stroked Sam's cheek. "Are you still nervous about meeting Dad?"

Sam winced. "Of course I am. He's nice on the phone, but I'm the man deflowering his baby boy. He has to hate me."

Teague arched a brow. "Deflowering his baby boy? Feeling a little dramatic today?"

Sam snickered. "Okay, so I'm sexing up his much-used son."

"Wow, there's no in between there for you, huh?"

Sam slapped his shoulder, body shaking with laughter. "I love you, Tee. You know that, right?"

Teague smiled and pressed his forehead to Sam's. "I suspect you love my *much-used* ass."

Sam laughed harder. "Shut up and tell me you love me again."

Teague carefully rolled their bodies until Sam lay on top of him. "I love you, Sam. More than I ever thought I could love another person. You're my home and my future, and I can't wait to spend my life with you."

Sam sighed, eyes softening. "Good boy."

LATER THAT MORNING, Teague tugged Nile's new hunter green sweater onto the cat. Binks nestled in his hair as usual, and Teague did his best to keep his head still so the bird would be comfortable.

Puff watched him from his heated terrarium in the

corner. It was a very cold October day, so Teague's bearded dragon would be staying with his heat lamp.

"Reuben's here with the food," Sam said, hobbling into the kitchen. "Oh my god, this is really happening."

"Calm down, hambone." Mia sat in a padded rocking chair next to the window. Merle and Journey both slept on her lap. "Today's going to go perfectly. The whole damn town is coming, and you know they'll do their best by y'all."

Teague nodded. Today was the official opening of the Furever Home Sanctuary, and he should be nervous. The place was going to cost a fortune to run, and he had already taken in fifteen goats. It was getting very real, very quickly.

"Nugget, Moose, and Ernie finished dressing the goats," Sam said, bending down to scratch Orville's ears. "The Pajama Party Barn is officially ready to go. Ernie and Gramps are running the show there."

Teague grinned. That right there was why he wasn't nervous at all. Sam and Mia knew everyone in this tiny town and had called in backup to make the day unforgettable.

"Beautiful," Morris squawked as he flew toward Sam.

Sam held out his arm. "Hello, my love. You're going to have so much fun today. We're setting you up with Binks, Aunt Mia, and the parakeets in the music room. You all get to serenade the guests."

Binks whistled sharply, and the dogs and pigs ran toward Teague, almost knocking him over. Moose carried the hamster ball in his mouth. Leroy and Barnaby watched him from inside.

"Damn it, Binks," he said, barely staying upright. "Now I have to give them treats. You're going to make them fat."

Binks tweeted innocently.

Mia stood and settled Merle and Journey onto the floor. "I'm going to get my fiddle ready. We rehearsed the playlist last night."

Teague hugged Mia before she could shuffle out of the room. He had come home many times to find the woman playing a slow tune with the birds gathered around her, doing their best to sing along. "Thanks, Mia. I appreciate your help with this."

She rolled her eyes. "Like it's a hardship to play songs with the birds."

Binks hopped over to settle onto the top of Mia's head, curled up against her messy gray bun.

Mia smiled and gently patted the bird. "Come on, Morris. Leave your sweetheart and let's get to work."

Morris gave Sam one more coy look, then flew after Mia.

Teague finished handing out treats, then smoothed down his hair. Binks always messed it up. *At least he didn't shit on me today.*

Sam wrapped his arms around Teague. "So, Justin told me he overheard Doc Grover saying something about some donkeys moving in with us."

Teague gave him a kiss. "My first official rescues. Doc says Journey and the goats don't count because they're part of the family now."

Sam rolled his eyes. "Any animal you take in will be part of the family. That man just wants to soften you up for something big."

"Hello, hello." Timothy's voice came from the living room. The herd of dogs and pigs ran to the front of the house to greet him.

Tortellini slowly moved past them, Mimi on his back. The kitten was starting to get big, but fortunately, the tortoise was sturdy.

"It's time," Sam said ominously. "Morris isn't even here for support."

Teague bent down and picked up Noodle. "Here, you can have the queen. She'll protect you."

Sam took Noodle from him and slowly headed for the living room.

Teague gave Charlie and Niles a look. "Can you believe he thinks Dad won't like him?"

Charlie meowed softly, and Niles ignored them to go get a drink of water.

By the time Teague reached the front room, Timothy was hugging Sam. While the kitchen was still a seventies nightmare, they had recently remodeled the front sitting room and the living room. The old wallpaper was gone and fresh, creamy white paint covered the walls. The hardwood floors had been sanded and refinished, and new furniture filled the room.

"I'm so happy to finally meet you. I knew Teague was crazy about you the day he first told me about this amazing omega he had met. He couldn't stop talking about how funny and smart you were."

"Dad," Teague whined. "Don't tell him that."

Sam gave him a smug look over Timothy's shoulder. "You looooved me."

Mia chuckled as she set her fiddle case down. "Sam was the same way. He kept comparing that nasty boyfriend of his to Teague, and let me tell you, the boyfriend didn't come out on top."

"Aunt Mia." Sam scowled.

Teague smirked. "What's wrong, Sam? Don't want to admit you looooved me too?"

Timothy finally let Sam go and shook his finger at Teague. "Watch it, young man. You don't want to chase this one away."

Dennis smiled from the doorway. "I don't think there's much chance of that happening, pookie bear. Look at how besotted they are."

Teague forced himself to stop smiling at Sam. "I don't know what you mean."

Dennis gave him a knowing look, then went to Mia's side. "I hear you're in charge of the music for this gathering. May I help?"

Mia winked at him. "Sure thing, cutie. Can you help me get the birds to the smaller barn out back? That's where we're setting up."

"Certainly." Dennis gave her a little bow, then bent to pick up her case.

Timothy rolled his eyes. "I better go keep an eye on those two. I'd like to keep my husband, thank you very much. By the way, I saw a nice young man directing guests to the back. A few of the sponsors are already here."

"We'll go meet them," Teague said, nerves finally making an appearance.

"Put your coat on, Aunt Mia," Sam called out. "It's cold outside."

A moment later, Mia and the two men were gone, and Sam and Teague were alone again.

Sam watched him, smiling. "Finally feeling the moment?"

Teague nodded. "Dennis invited six of his super-rich friends to the opening. They're all big sponsors. Dad donated the most so far, but these people have already given me a lot of money. I don't want to mess this up. There are so many animals that need me."

Sam smoothed his hands over Teague's shoulders. "You have no reason to worry. These people will see exactly what I do. A brilliant veterinarian with a kind heart that wants to love the animals no one else will. They'll see how much work you've done to the property and how happy the goats and the rest of our pets are. We'll show them your dream, Tee, and they won't be able to resist it."

Teague cupped Sam's cheek. "They better not see my dream, Sam. I'm not sharing you with them."

Sam flushed, eyes widening. "What?"

Teague ran a thumb over Sam's full bottom lip. "I've wanted this sanctuary for a long time, but there's nothing I want more in life than you. You make this dream of mine complete, and I swear you have no idea how important you are to me. When I say I love you, Sam, I mean I need you more than the air I breathe."

Sam's eyes watered, and he leaned into Teague's touch. "I need you too. You're my person, Teague. I love you so much, and I promise I'll spend the rest of my life making sure you know it."

Teague gave Sam a soft kiss, feeling the promise in his words settle into his bones.

CHAPTER 13

Sam chuckled as he watched Teague and one of Dennis's wealthy friends play with Wilbur and Orville. The two men kicked a beach ball between them and laughed as the two miniature pigs chased it.

Moose leaned against Sam's good leg, seemingly happy as he watched the crowd around them.

"Need to sit?" Reuben asked from his other side. Sam's friend had surprised him by actually leaving the kitchen. Reuben didn't do well in crowds of people.

His youngest son, Maury, sat on his hip, chewing on his fist. The baby's wild red curls stuck up in every direction.

Sam squeezed the handle of his crutch. "It's nice to be up."

"Something wrong?" Reuben leaned against the side of the barn and snuggled his son closer.

Sam was quiet for a moment as he looked around. People from town walked between the barns and the tents. Justin ran the food tent and was currently handing out all the delicious food The Irish Rose had donated. Zoe and her husband, Gib, served coffee, tea, and apple cider from another tent, and Yeo and his husband worked in the costume tent with Nugget, Percy, and Niles.

"Sam?" Reuben said.

"Do you think Teague and I are moving too fast?" Sam absently played with Moose's ears. "Everything feels so *right*, and I don't know if I should trust it. It never felt like this with Brett."

He purposely didn't think about the peanut growing inside him. He had tried not to think about the doctor's news, but it was hard to do that when Teague was hovering over him because of his leg.

His boyfriend was good at taking care of others, and Sam could easily see them building a family. Hell, they had settled into living with each other easily enough.

"Trust your gut." Reuben gave him a small smile. "You've been his friend for a long time. Maybe he was meant to be your alpha all this time."

Sam absently settled a hand on his abdomen. "He's the best person I know."

Reuben grunted and eyed Sam's belly. "He'd better be."

Sam flushed and moved his hand. "Thanks for cooking all that food. Timothy said that we've gotten a lot of donations from people in town, and I know your food's what brought them here."

Reuben shrugged. "Goats in pajamas are irresistible."

Sam watched another group of smiling people leave the Pajama Party Barn. "You may be right. Okay, maybe I do need to sit down."

Reuben nodded and followed him into the music barn. It took a moment to find a couple empty seats, because open space was crowded, but Reuben found one and carried it to him, settling it near the door.

Sam sat down and reached for Maury. "Please?"

Reuben kissed his son's curls and handed him to Sam.

Sam held the baby and watched Aunt Mia and a couple of her friends, including Doc Grover, play their instruments while the birds sang along. Teague's herd weren't typically shy animals, but Morris was a little more skittish than usual. The parakeets tweeted along happily, and Binks was content on top of Mia's head.

Doc Grover did something fancy on his cello and the crowd clapped. They looked enthralled by the informal concert, and Sam was surprised. He knew why *he* thought it was adorable.

Moose settled at his side, huffing as he plopped down.

"I'll get you some food," Reuben whispered.

Sam gave him a suspicious look. "Wait. Did Teague ask you to babysit me?"

Reuben gave him a guilty look. "You're hurt."

Sam rolled his eyes. "I'm okay. Just for that, I'm keeping Maury with me all day, or at least until he needs a diaper change. Go away."

Reuben chuckled. "I'll be back with food."

"DAD, you don't have to donate for today too." Teague gave his dad an exasperated look. "You're a formal sponsor, so you've already pledged an annual amount."

Sam laughed when Timothy gave his son a dirty look. "It's my husband's money, and I'll do what I want with it."

"Hey now," Dennis interrupted. "That's your money, pookie bear. I have my own donation to make."

Teague threw his hands up. "You two are impossible. You already invited your friends here, Dennis. You don't have to do more."

Dennis wrapped an arm around Timothy's shoulders.

"We'll be gone for months on our cruise, and this is the last time we'll get to see you. Let us spoil you a bit."

"Please?" Timothy asked, fluttering his eyes.

Sam laughed again. "If he doesn't let you, just give me the money and *I'll* donate it. I don't need his permission."

Teague growled and pulled him onto his lap. "Don't enable them."

Sam leaned against him and fought back a yawn. "Don't tell me what to do."

"Shit, you must be exhausted." Teague hugged him. "Let's get you to bed."

Sam scowled. "I'll go to bed when I'm ready."

Timothy giggled. "On that note, Dennis and I better get to the bed and breakfast. We'll see you in the morning before we leave."

The older omega leaned over and kissed Teague's forehead. "I'm proud of you, son. This is going to be a wonderful sanctuary for all those pets and farm animals that need love."

Sam smiled at Teague's flushed cheeks.

"Thanks, Dad." Teague cleared his throat. "See you for breakfast."

They left and Sam and Teague stayed where they were for a while. Aunt Mia had already gone to bed. She had taken plenty of breaks all day, but it had still been exhausting. The pets were already asleep. They had played hard during the opening and needed some rest.

"We raised a lot of money today." Teague shook his head. "Not counting the donations from Dad and Dennis's friends, we raised over two thousand dollars. More importantly, a lot of people volunteered their time. Sheriff McKenzie even donated a ton of goat feed."

Sam rubbed his face against Teague's shoulder. "Hobson Hills has some good people in it."

"Damn right it does." Teague stroked a hand over his

cheek. "I'm glad we live here. It's a good place to raise our pets."

Sam snorted. "Raise our pets, huh?"

Teague shrugged. "That's less scary than talking about having kids, isn't it?"

"What's scary about having a baby?" Sam asked, worry churning in his gut.

"I'm trying not to scare you off here," Teague whispered against his ear. "I love you, Sam, and I fully expect us to build a life here. Kids too if you're willing."

Sam buried his face against Teague's neck, hating the tears that ran down his cheeks.

"Sammie? What's wrong?" Teague tilted his face up and gave him a concerned look. "We don't have to rush anything, and if you don't want kids, that's okay."

Sam couldn't stop the laughter that bubbled up. His body shook as he laughed hard.

"Okay, I'm really worried here."

Sam looked up. "I'm pregnant, Tee. The doctor told me at the hospital last week. They run some tests automatically, and that's one of them."

Teague's eyes widened and his face went slack. "Pregnant?"

Sam nodded, his uncertainty returning. "I'm still wrapping my head around it. It's really early yet, but there's a person growing inside me. Isn't that fucked-up?"

Teague gently stroked Sam's abdomen. "Shit, fuck, damn."

"So eloquent." Sam chuckled nervously. "Okay, really, though. What are you thinking?"

Teague blinked, still looking dazed. "I'm thinking I'm the luckiest person in the entire world. I get you *and* our baby."

Sam swallowed hard. "Good. That's good. I'm so scared, Teague. A baby is a huge deal."

"Hey, now." Teague pressed his forehead to Sam's. "We're in this together. We can handle it."

Sam nodded, taking deep breaths. "Okay. We can. We can do this." He looked up. "Let's wait to tell Aunt Mia and your dads, okay? It's really early in."

"Sure." Teague hugged him tightly. "Wait, you said my *dads*."

Sam snorted, feeling his panic start to ease as they changed the subject. "Dennis is so your dad. You need to accept that and move on already."

Teague hummed to himself for a moment. "Dennis is a good dad."

Sam smiled against Teague's neck. *Teague will be a good dad too.*

A few weeks later, Teague, Nugget, and Percy fed and watered the goats in what he had started to call *the goat barn*. Six more goats had made their way to Teague's sanctuary, along with two donkeys, three more pigs, and a very grumpy rooster.

Nugget wore his favorite giraffe hat today and took his time saying hello to each of the goats in the open pasture that connected to the back of their barn. They were a mix of breeds, but managed to get along well. Most had been owned by one person who had treated them well, but had gotten overwhelmed by the amount of work it took to care for so many animals.

Percy stayed at Teague's side as he shoveled goat shit into a wheelbarrow. In a lot of ways, running his sanctuary was harder work than running his own clinic, but it was also a hell of a lot of fun.

"What kind of ring do you think Sam will like?" he asked Percy. "Will he even want one? Some people don't like rings and I've never seen him wear one."

"Woof." Percy rolled over to inspect Tilda, the one goat

that had decided to stay inside the barn today. She wedged her head between the rails and sniffed Percy's face.

"Do you think he'll even say yes if I propose?" Teague huffed and moved to the next pile of crap. "I don't want him to think I'm proposing just because of the baby. I love him and want to take this next step with him. Dad and I are more alike than I thought. I was worried when he came home married to Dennis, but if I had met Sam on a cruise, I would have done my best to make him mine too."

His phone rang from his back pocket, and he took off his gloves and checked the number. *Henry?* Dennis's youngest kid wasn't exactly Teague or Timothy's biggest fan, so it was a surprise to see his number on the screen.

"Hello," Teague said cautiously. He had spoken to his dad earlier in the day, so he knew there wasn't something wrong with Timothy or Dennis.

"You greedy son of a bitch," Henry said, furious. "Did you think we wouldn't find out?"

Teague made a face and sat down on a wooden bench he'd put in so Sam could rest his leg while visiting the goats. "Henry, I really don't have time for temper tantrums. Just tell me what the hell is wrong."

"You know what you did," Henry said, voice rising in anger. "You and that gold-digging whore dad of yours didn't realize that Mr. Lavardi's paralegal is dating Audrey's personal trainer."

Teague rubbed the bridge of his nose. "I swear to god, if you insult my dad one more time, I'll fucking fly to New York and kick your ass. It's been years. Move the hell on and accept that Dennis is happy with my dad."

"Don't try to distract me." Henry's growl was kind of adorable, but Teague didn't think he'd appreciate hearing that. "Jerry told Paula everything, and she told Audrey. We know Dad changed his will."

Teague sighed. "That makes one of us then. Is that even legal? Doesn't that breach a client's privacy or something like that?"

"I'm sure you'd like us to never know that Dad left millions to that stupid animal sanctuary of yours. It probably doesn't even exist, and Dad fell for all Timothy's lies about you." Henry sounded like he was about to hyperventilate. "We won't let you get away with this. We aren't going to let you take advantage of our dad."

Teague blinked, tears welling. "He left millions to Furever Home Sanctuary? Really?"

"Like you didn't know." Henry huffed. "That on top of your portion of his estate is more than any of the rest of us are getting. Dad wouldn't do that unless you tricked him."

"He left me a portion of his estate?" Teague shook his head. "Why would he do that?"

"It's an *equal* portion and you're not even his child." Henry growled again. "As soon as he gets back from that stupid cruise, we'll straighten this out, so don't think you've won, asshole."

The call ended, and Teague stared at his phone for a while.

Percy rolled to him and rested his head on Teague's knee.

"Dennis put me in his will." Teague swallowed hard. "Holy shit, Percy. Sam was right. Dennis really is my dad."

"Woof."

Teague shook himself. "Yeah, you're right. It doesn't matter because he and Dad had best never die anyway. I'm so yelling at him when he gets back too. There's no reason for him to leave that much to me if he's donating to the sanctuary too."

He had just finished cleaning the barn when his phone rang again. "Percy, it better be Sam calling for a bout of phone sex. That's the only reason to answer the phone at this point."

It wasn't Sam.

"Brett." Teague was proud that his tone didn't give away his frustration.

"Sam texted me this morning and said to stop calling him." Brett sounded shocked. "Did he have head damage in the accident? I thought it was just a broken arm."

"Broken *leg,* jackass." Okay, that definitely didn't hide his frustration. "Sam isn't coming back to you. He and I are dating now."

"I *knew* you wanted him," Brett said smugly. "I saw the way you watched my omega. Listen, he may be upset right now, but his head will clear and he'll come back to me. He's just vulnerable from the accident."

"Are you for real?" Teague gave Percy and Tilda a disbelieving look. "This guy actually thinks the only reason Sam doesn't want to be with him is because he got shook up in the accident. What the actual fuck?"

"Who are your talking to? Never mind, it doesn't matter." Brett sounded annoyed. "I'll call Sam next week, and we'll see what's actually going on. I feel sorry for you, Teague. You probably do care for Sam, but he loves me and you know it."

The call ended and Teague rolled his eyes. "What did Sam ever see in that guy?"

Percy licked Tilda's face and the goat backed away from the fence.

Teague tucked his phone away and whistled. "Come on, Nugget. Enough goat time. We need to check on the donkeys."

Nugget and Percy played with each other as they walked the freshly paved path to the larger barn. The weather was getting cooler, and Aunt Mia swore she felt snow coming, but at that moment, it was a beautiful autumn day. The trees in the nearby woods had a beautiful variety of red, yellow, and orange leaves, and the crisp air felt good against his sweaty skin.

Aunt Mia's house looked nice against the backdrop of the pastures surrounding it. *Home*, he thought. Teague could easily imagine carrying his child on his back from the house as they made the rounds to take care of the animals.

"Guys, what if Sam really does go back to Brett?"

Nugget and Percy stopped and turned to stare at him. Percy woofed softly, and Teague swore he was calling Teague an idiot in dog.

"He was with him for years, and he *did* love him," Teague pointed out.

Nugget moved to press against his legs and gave him a soulful look.

"I know he says he loves me too, but we've only been together a few months."

Nugget shook his head and ran with Percy to the other barn.

"No need to be rude." Teague grunted and hurried to follow them.

The two donkeys, Levi and Sunflower, had come from separate homes, but the two of them had both been neglected. Teague had them on a good diet and checked them over daily, so he had hope they'd do well eventually.

Sunflower watched him from her stall. She was the friendlier of the two.

"Hey, beautiful." Teague took the organic treat from his pocket and slowly approached her. He held his hand out, palm open and let her take her time in nuzzling around for the treat.

Levi was terrified of people, but he at least liked the dogs.

Teague balanced a treat on Percy's head, and the pit bull made his way to Levi's stall. The donkey watched Teague from the back for a while, then slowly approached. He leaned over the door and gently nuzzled Percy's face before nipping at the treat.

Teague chuckled lightly and left them to visit while he checked on their newest resident, Bucky the rooster.

The Silver Ameraucana rooster was a beautiful fella, but he made no secret that he didn't care for people. The rooster's new home was a little small, but he was still recovering from surgery.

Teague had made a small wood and wire cage for him near the donkeys so he wouldn't get lonely.

"How you doing, handsome?" Teague kept his voice gentle and approached the cage slowly. He grinned when he saw Bucky up and walking around. "Look at you!"

Bucky's previous owner's son was a nasty jerk and had taken a lot of joy in hurting the chicken. Three days ago, the boy's mother had shown up with Bucky in a cat carrier. Her son had smashed one of the rooster's legs, and she didn't know what to do about it. Even assuming Bucky lived, he clearly couldn't go back home with her.

Teague and Doc Grover had worked together to amputate Bucky's leg and had created a makeshift prosthesis for the rooster. Teague knew a lot of his colleagues wouldn't have bothered with so much work for a chicken, but Doc Grover was different.

"You're up and walking, Bucky." Teague grabbed his phone and took a picture, quickly sending it to Doc Grover. "You're doing good. How about some mealworms?"

By the time he shut the barn door behind him, it was well past lunch time. "Damn it, guys. Sam will kill me if he finds out I skipped lunch again."

"Doc Walsh," a voice called out. Hannah Wilson, one of his neighbors and absolute favorite volunteer, ran toward him from the house. She waved a bagged sandwich in her hand. "Aunt Mia said you didn't have lunch."

Orville and Wilbur ran behind her, tails swishing happily.

He waited for her to catch up, then gratefully took the sandwich. "I thought you were working at the veterinarian clinic today."

"Doc Grover said it was slow today, so I'm here to play with the pigs." Hannah grinned. "Are they still in the back pasture? Orville, Wilbur, and I have some games planned."

Teague quickly swallowed a bite of his sandwich and nodded. "They're still there. Will you give them a few apples?"

"You bet." She ran past him, her long braid whipping behind her. The teenager was always so full of energy and smiles. It made him feel old.

Wilbur and Orville didn't even bother saying hello. They just followed Hannah.

The other pigs had needed a few days to adjust to being around the miniatures. All three had the same story. Their separate owners had bought them from someone claiming they were miniatures, then were surprised when they kept growing. Now, the three were far too big and messy to be house pigs.

Teague finished his sandwich, then headed to the stables. With Gramps and Tomás's help, the barns were in good shape, so now his focus was on the stables.

"Time to get back to work, boys," Teague said, grinning at Nugget and Percy. "Forget rude stepsiblings and dumbass exes. We have more important things to do."

CHAPTER 15

Sam sighed happily as he scratched his bare leg. His cast had been off for a week now, and he was so damn happy.

Justin opened the office door and looked inside. "Are you scratching your leg again? Do you really need to do that in my office? Can't you go to the bathroom?"

Sam shrugged, cheeks heating up. He liked using Justin's office, because he could sit and take a little nap on his break too. He couldn't do that in the bathroom.

Justin gave him a suspicious look. "Reuben told me, but I didn't believe him. Let's see, your appetite has been off, you get sick almost every afternoon at two, and you've been taking naps. Sam, are you pregnant?"

Sam winced. "It's still really early."

Justin gave him a sympathetic look and closed the door behind him. "How far along are you?"

"Almost three months now." Sam made a face. "It still doesn't feel real."

Justin knelt in front of him and took his hands. "Hey, you

aren't alone here. I imagine Teague knows and is happy about it. Your aunt adores you and will spoil this baby rotten. Then you have us. Reuben and I especially can help out if you need anything. I'm a good babysitter and my Ronnie likes having other babies around. Hell, Tanner and I were thinking of having another, so this will be good practice for her to be a big sister."

Sam's eyes watered. "You're the best boss ever."

"You say that now, but you have to clean out the freezer tomorrow." Justin grinned. "You'll be cursing me plenty then."

Sam laughed. "Gee, thanks."

"Let me know when you make the announcement, so I don't have to keep it a secret. I'm throwing the baby shower too. Trust me. You want all the diapers anyone and everyone gives you."

Sam hugged him. "Thanks."

Justin's arms wrapped around him and Sam hugged him back. "That's what friends are for. Now, take the afternoon off. North came in early, because he knew my little brother was stopping by and he wants to flirt. I'll put him on the dishes."

Sam snorted. "I'll take it. I could use a longer nap."

"Growing babies takes a lot of energy," Justin said, helping him stand. "Go home and nap."

A few moments later, Sam bundled up in his coat, hat, gloves, and scarf. It was only a short walk to his car, but he hated being chilled. His new car handled the icy roads a lot better than his old one, which was a good thing since December had decided to be extra cold this year.

When he pulled into the driveway, he saw a car he didn't recognize. It was expensive, but he thought it might be a rental.

"Aunt Mia, I'm home," he called out as he opened the

door. The herd descended on him, and he took the time to greet and pet everyone.

Morris settled on his arm as he finally looked around the living room.

Mia sat in her recliner with Merle in her lap. Luna and Dove, as usual, lounged behind her.

Sam frowned. "Where's Journey?"

Mia smirked and pointed at the young omega sitting on the couch. The man hugged Journey to his chest and was cooing at the Pomeranian mix. Journey's hair still hadn't filled in, though Teague and Doc Grover had been able to treat his fungal infection. He looked a little funny, but he was a sweet dog.

"This is Henry, Teague's youngest brother," Mia said, sounding amused.

"Stepbrother," Henry corrected, looking up. "If that."

Noodle watched the omega closely, blue eyes cold and hard. *Please don't attack him*, Sam thought, wanting to laugh. Charlie, Niles, and Mimi didn't seem to mind the young man, but Noodle was always tough on strangers.

"Teague isn't here right now," Sam said, yawning. "He's working at the clinic today."

Henry sniffed. "Of course he's conveniently not home. I'm here to check out his so-called animal sanctuary." He looked around. "I see plenty of animals, but I don't know where the donations Dad's been making are going. This place is a dump."

Sam sighed. He really wanted that damn nap. "This is our home, not the sanctuary."

Henry flushed and gave Mia an apologetic look. "Oh, I'm sorry."

She waved his concern away. "I should show you the kitchen. That will really make you appreciate what we've done with the living room."

Sam snorted. "Shag carpet in a kitchen, Aunt Mia. What were you thinking?"

She chuckled. "It was the seventies, sweet potato. I wasn't thinking."

"Come on." Sam patted Henry's shoulder and settled Morris on one of his perches. "I'll show you the sanctuary. You're staying for dinner, right? I'm making a pot of white chicken chili. It's the best on a cold day like this."

Henry blinked. "You're inviting me to dinner?"

"Don't worry," Aunt Mia called out as they went outside. "The dining room doesn't have shag carpet."

Henry's cheeks turned pink. "I really am sorry."

"Don't worry about it. You really should see the kitchen." Sam eyed Journey. "Are you going to set him down?"

Henry pouted. "He doesn't want to go down. He told me he wants to stay with me forever and wear all the cute little outfits I'll buy him."

Sam stifled a laugh. "Ahh, I see. Well, he likes visiting the others, so come on."

Nugget, Percy, Moose, and Lily pushed out the door with them, happy to romp around in the snow. Orville and Wilbur were content to stay inside in front of the fireplace.

Henry looked at the barn in the distance. "We have to walk there?"

Sam rolled his eyes. "You have a coat."

"It's just so far."

"Cardio is good for you." Sam shut the door behind him and slipped his gloves back on. "Now, we have goats, donkeys, pigs, and chickens in the barns. We also got a llama yesterday, but he's still acclimating, so we'll leave him alone. You might see five cats hanging around the barn. Don't be mad if they don't come up to be petted. They're half-feral, so we're giving them the run of the barns."

Henry's eyes widened. "I thought this place just opened."

"It did, but we'll fill up fast." Sam winced. "I dread the day when Teague will have to turn an animal away. It *will* happen. That's life and we only have so much space. It's going to break his heart."

Henry frowned. "He can adopt animals out, right?"

"Ideally, but there's usually a reason the animal is here and not a shelter." Sam shook his head. "Why do you care anyway? I thought you hated Teague."

Henry's mouth thinned. "I just don't want someone taking advantage of my dad."

"You honestly think Timothy isn't head over heels in love with Dennis?" Sam arched a brow. "Have you seen them together?"

Henry scowled. "It's obviously just physical attraction. Papa always said Dad had a wandering eye."

Sam frowned. "Dennis cheated on your dad?"

Henry shrugged. "Papa said he did, but the divorce lawyers never brought it up in court."

"You think they would have if Dennis *had* cheated?" Sam asked, curious. Dennis hadn't seemed the type, but honestly, Sam wasn't always a good judge of character.

Henry snorted. "They definitely would have. Papa had to fight for his settlement."

"I wonder why?" Sam said, smiling when Moose barreled into a pile of snow. "Dennis seems like a fair-minded guy, but really, what do I know?"

Henry waved his words away. "It doesn't matter. Dad just isn't the type to be generous, but Timothy and his son have him wrapped around their little fingers."

"Have you talked to him about it?" Sam asked when they reached the goat barn.

"I called Teague and told him." Henry huffed. "That's why I'm here. Follow along."

"I don't mean Teague," Sam said, trying not to roll his eyes again. He didn't want them to get stuck, and Henry's tantrums would actually do it. "I meant have you talked to Dennis about this?"

Henry gave him a shocked look. "Of course not. That's not the kind of conversation you have with your father."

Sam closed his eyes. "What does that even mean?"

"I'm not going to drag up Dad's sordid affairs over lunch," Henry said, rolling *his* eyes. "We talk about my trust fund, the most recent society gossip, and horse racing."

"So, nothing of substance. Got it." Sam shook his head. "I'm going to talk about everything with my baby. That's all there is to it."

Henry froze behind him. "Your baby? Are you pregnant?"

Sam winced and opened the barn door. "Get inside."

Henry followed him in. "Is it Teague's? Does your aunt know?"

"Of course it's Teague's," Sam said, annoyed. "It's still early on, so I haven't told Aunt Mia, but I really need to. I'll start showing soon and she's sharp as cheese. She'll notice."

"Smart as cheese?" Henry snickered. "You're so strange."

Sam grabbed the bag of treats and tossed them at Henry. "Oh hush and give the goats their treats."

Henry caught them with his free hand. "I can't. I have to hold my little darling Journey."

Sam took Journey from Henry and pointed at the goats. "Behold their existence and give them treats."

Henry frowned, then turned to the goats. They all watched him carefully, well aware of what was in the treat bag. "My god, you have a lot of goats."

"More arrive every week." Sam checked their water and feed while he was there. "Teague named them all. I can't keep them straight, but he can tell you each of their names and personalities."

Sam chuckled. "Audrey *hates* goats. They terrified her

during one trip to the petting zoo when we were kids. Sterling had to swoop in and save her, because this cute little goat was chewing on her dress. She's loathed them ever since."

"Well, it's a good thing she's not here." Sam crossed his arms. Teague's army of goats really were sweet. Mostly.

~

LATER THAT NIGHT, Sam washed dishes while Henry and Teague tried to talk Journey into wearing a sweater.

"You can do it, sweetness," Henry cooed. "Just think of how adorable you'll look."

"It'll keep you warm, Journey, and you hate the cold," Teague added, trying to hold the wiggling dog still.

"One paw in," Henry said, excited. "Almost there."

Aunt Mia chuckled. "I think those two are going to be okay. Teague has a soft spot for people who love animals."

"I can't believe Henry's staying here for the week," Sam said quietly, "I thought for sure he'd go for the bed and breakfast."

"I think Teague won him over by introducing him to each goat." Mia chuckled. "That man of yours is something special."

"He's my alpha." Sam's mind wandered, and he imagined Teague smiling down at an infant nestled in his arms.

"What's going on with you?" she asked, arching a brow. She sat at the table, Merle keeping her feet warm and Luna snuggling with her. "You've been acting shifty ever since your accident."

Sam bit his lip, thinking about how well both Justin and Henry had taken the news that he was pregnant. He didn't really understand why he was afraid to tell his aunt. "I'm pregnant," he blurted out. "Almost three months pregnant."

Mia blinked, lips parting, but no words coming out.

"Do you hate me?" he whispered. "For not being responsible? You taught me better, but I didn't even think about protection."

Mia snorted. "Clearly, Teague didn't either. It takes two, tater tot." She gave him a soft look. "I could never hate you, especially not for something like this. Are you happy about the baby?"

He shrugged. "Yeah? I want kids with Teague, but this was so unexpected. I just don't want anyone to be mad at me."

Mia huffed and stood up, gently nudging Merle off her feet and setting Luna down. "Come give me a hug, peanut. I'm gonna be a great-great-aunt. Damn, I'm old."

Sam laughed, relief filling him as he hugged his aunt. "You're fucking ancient."

CHAPTER 16

Teague nuzzled the back of Sam's neck, his hand resting on his omega's slightly rounded abdomen. "I can't wait until Dad and Dennis get back from the cruise. Dad is going to cry when we tell him about the baby. He's wanted grandkids for a while."

Sam leaned back into him and deftly slipped the omelet from the pan to a plate. "He won't think I'm trying to trap you in a relationship?"

Teague snorted. "Dad knows you, Sammie. You worry about what other people think too much."

Sam groaned. "I really do. I can't believe I thought Aunt Mia would be mad."

"Me neither," Mia said from her usual padded seat at the table. "I need a refill, Teague, and bring me my omelet."

"Bossy old woman." Sam handed Teague the plated omelet. "Better feed her before she eats Moose."

Mia eyed the large dog currently sleeping under the table. "He'd make a good roast."

Teague grabbed the coffee pot and refilled her cup, then set her plate in front of her. "Poor Moose."

Sam laughed, then set a plated omelet in front of Teague's seat before going back to the stove to finish his own. "So, Aunt Mia is taking it easy and napping today. What are you doing?"

Teague rolled his shoulders and poured Sam a glass of chocolate milk to go with his breakfast. His omega was really missing his lattes. "The goats get their checkups today, and I need to give Levi a good brushing. His winter coat is coming in thick. Then, there's the new pig. I'm going to check her over to be sure, but I'm almost certain she's pregnant. I swear, we're turning into a goat and pig farm."

"I'll visit Bucky before I leave for work. He needs some extra loving." Sam sat down and dug into his omelet. "I think we should move him to the utility room."

Mia almost snorted her coffee. "You can't keep a rooster in the house."

Sam glared at his aunt. "Bucky is my special boy, just like Morris. He belongs with me."

Morris stared at Mia from the back of Sam's chair. "My beautiful love. My beautiful love."

Sam sniffed and sipped his milk. "Thank you, my darling."

Teague hid his smile. "Bucky has his hens to watch over though."

People had been dropping off chickens periodically the entire time they'd been open. Mostly they were roosters, but there were several hens too. Teague had created separate coops with one rooster and two hens to keep the fighting down. Bucky had taken to Mabel and Peggy Sue.

"He's *my* rooster," Sam said, pouting.

Teague slipped one of his pieces of toast to Sam's plate and pushed the strawberry jam closer to his omega. "Where would Bucky be happier?"

Sam gave him a dirty look. "Don't go logical on me, Doctor Dolittle."

Mia laughed. "You two are a hoot. Now, shut up and eat your breakfast. I want more eggs for lunch, and that means you need to go check the coops before work, Sam. You can visit with Bucky then."

"She's *so* bossy today," Sam said, voice low.

"I heard that." She stole the last piece of Teague's toast. "Just for that, I need you to stop at Farm Fresh on the way home tonight and get me a loaf of apple bread."

Sam bowed his head and twirled his hand. "As you wish, my queen."

Teague cleaned off the table and did dishes, while Sam showered and dressed for work. It still felt strange to not rush out the door to go to work each morning. Instead, he usually did the morning feedings, then had a leisurely breakfast with Sam and Mia.

He looked over his shoulder when the dogs and pigs started sitting up. *Then there's Henry.*

Henry yawned as he slowly made his way into the kitchen, Journey cuddled in his arms as usual. "Hello, my angels. Do you need your morning treats? Uncle Henry will take care of you."

He shared an amused look with Mia. Henry was still staying with them a month after he'd arrived. Teague didn't mind as much as he had thought he would, since Henry pitched in with the sanctuary. The younger man had even filled in serving tables at the pub when they had been short-staffed last week.

Sam came back in, fighting back a yawn. He laughed when Wilbur devoured his treat, then pushed his way back in front of Henry for another. "Uncle Henry only gives one treat each, Wilbur."

Teague fought back a grin. Sam and Henry got along really well and had become surprisingly good friends.

"Come on, Henry. Bundle up and let's go get eggs, so Aunt

Mia doesn't exile us from her kingdom." Sam tugged on Henry's arm. "Bucky needs us."

Henry laughed and set the box of treats down. "On it."

After the two left, Teague sat back down at the table.

Mia eyed him as she sipped her third cup of coffee. "You're only a little smiley and happy today. What's wrong?"

Teague shrugged. "Nothing."

She arched a brow. "Enjoying working with Doc Grover?"

Teague rubbed his chin. "Well, he *is* excessively cheerful all the time, but I do like the man."

"The rest of the clinic staff are decent, aren't they?" she asked.

Teague nodded. "Hannah's my favorite. She may just be a volunteer, but I've never met someone so full of determination."

"She'll own that clinic one day." Mia smiled softly. "She's a sweet girl. Now, tell me what's wrong."

"I want to marry Sam." Teague leaned forward. "Do you think he'll think it's because of the baby? Should I wait to propose until after they're born?"

Mia chuckled. "I swear you two overthink everything. Just talk to him and find out what he wants."

Teague shook his head. "That's just crazy talk, woman. Tortellini gives better advice."

She rolled her eyes. "I'm going to my room and talking to Merle and my cats. They're smarter company."

LATER THAT DAY, Teague patted Rollo's neck and led the llama back into his pen. Rollo preferred staying inside since the weather was officially colder than a polar bear's butt. "Thank you for being good for your check-up buddy. Tilda chewed on my sweater during hers. Can you believe that?"

The llama leaned over and settled his head on Teague's shoulder.

Teague hugged him and took some time to pamper the sweet guy. Rollo had come to him in pretty bad shape. Someone had found him in the woods, half-starved and scared. It wasn't clear if his owner had abandoned him or if he had just gotten out of his pen and then wandered off. Either way, he was Teague's now.

He had just fetched the broom and started to sweep out the goat barn, when the door slid open with a bang and an icy-cold wind blew inside.

Audrey Harrington stood in the doorway, her perfectly styled brown hair and fashionable winter attire very out of place in his barn.

"You son of a bitch." She slammed the barn door shut and stalked toward him. "What did you do to my brother? Henry says he's working in a pub now and he *likes* you."

Teague tilted his head. "Is he working at The Irish Rose now? I thought he was just filling in temporarily."

She scowled. "Whatever. Explain what the hell is going on. Now."

Teague sighed. "Listen, I don't have time for this. I need to sweep up here, then water the chickens."

Audrey stepped closer to him, her glare deepening. "Dad won't let you get away with this. I'm going to tell him everything when he gets home, and he'll throw your whore omega dad out on the street."

Teague's patience snapped. "Watch your fucking mouth. I don't care if you hate my dad, you'll treat him with respect when you're around me or you can get the fuck off my property."

She growled and moved to stand in front of him. "How dare you—"

Tilda slipped her head through the fence and started nibbling on the faux fox fur lining her expensive coat.

Audrey's eyes widened, and she shrieked loudly, wobbling on her heeled boots.

Tilda startled and immediately fainted, head slipping back from between the rails of the fence.

"I hate goats. I hate goats. I hate goats." Audrey danced in place, eyes filled with panic. "Keep them away."

Teague let out a relieved breath when Tilda stood back up. She was a fainting goat, so sometimes she fell over like that, but it always made him nervous when she did.

Audrey grabbed his coat. "Help me!"

Teague rolled his eyes. "Fucking hell, calm down." He finally looked her over, then immediately felt bad. She was genuinely scared. He wrapped his arms around her and hugged her close. "Hey, it's okay. The goats are behind that fence. They won't hurt you anyway. They're a friendly bunch."

"I hate goats." Her whole body trembled. "I hate them."

Teague walked her to the other side of the barn where Rollo stood watching them curiously. "What about llamas? Rollo here could use a good brushing. Will you help me?"

She nodded, face still stark white.

He led them into Rollo's stall and grabbed one of the brushes hanging up high. "Here you go. Rollo is a shy fella, but he's gentle. Just focus on his sides until he gets used to you."

She took the brush and slowly ran it over Rollo's thick fur.

Teague watched closely as Audrey slowly stopped trembling, and her brush strokes became more even and confident.

"Thank you," she whispered, cheeks pink. "I know it's stupid to be afraid of a goat."

Teague shrugged. "You should see me around spiders. I had to get an eighty-three-year-old woman to come kill one for me the other day."

Audrey snorted. "That's just embarrassing."

"So why hate goats?" Teague asked, stroking his brush over Rollo's long neck.

"There was an incident at a petting zoo." Audrey's face flushed again. "It was stupid. I know the goat wasn't trying to hurt me, but it was so close and had my dress in its teeth. I couldn't get away. Sterling rescued me while everyone else laughed."

"People can be shit sometimes," Teague said. He felt like shit himself. He probably would have been one of the people laughing.

She took a deep breath and let it out. "Why did you ask my dad to be put into his will?"

"I didn't." Teague sighed. "Listen, I didn't even ask him to donate to the sanctuary. He just did it. I *did* ask my dad to talk to him about finding sponsors when I first started. Dennis is good at schmoozing."

"Dad has a way of talking to people." Audrey bit her lip. "He's much better at that than Sterling."

"Really?" Teague's brows rose. "Dennis says Sterling is an excellent CEO of the investment firm."

"Oh, he is, but he relies on others to talk to the clients." Audrey tilted her head in concentration. "He's too... brusque would be the best word I suppose."

Teague grunted. He could understand that. He had been described as a little too abrupt himself.

"You really didn't ask him to put you in his will?" Audrey asked, giving him a hard look. "I understand him leaving a sizable portion to Timothy, since he's his little fling of the moment, but he's not related to you."

Teague's eyes narrowed. "Dad isn't Dennis's little

anything. He's his husband. They genuinely love one another."

"I find that hard to believe," Audrey said, scoffing. "Timothy puts on a good front, but he clearly isn't our kind of people."

Teague closed his eyes and took another breath. *Dennis kind of likes his daughter. No murdering her.* "Have you asked Dennis why he loves my dad?"

Audrey looked baffled. "Why would I do that? We don't talk about his affairs."

"What affairs?" Teague rolled his eyes. "He's with my dad constantly. Plus, believe me here, Dad would never put up with infidelity. He'd cut Dennis's balls off and leave him bleeding."

"Papa said Dad wasn't to be trusted." Audrey looked away. "He said Dad probably had another younger husband lined up."

Teague grunted again. "First, Dad and Dennis are almost the same age. I'd think if Dennis wanted a younger husband, he'd have married someone younger to start with. Second, and please don't take this the wrong way, but your omega dad isn't the best source of information on your Dad. The divorce wasn't amicable, was it?"

Audrey made a face. "It was horrible."

"So maybe your papa is hurting because Dennis remarried." Teague frowned. "Didn't your papa remarry?"

"Three times now." Audrey shrugged. "This last one seems more promising than the others."

Teague sighed. "Okay, so as soon as Dennis gets home, you and Henry need to sit down with him and have a fucking conversation. My dad doesn't deserve to be hated just because he dared to fall in love with your dad."

"People are shit. Isn't that what you said?" Audrey smiled coldly. "We can be as spiteful as we want."

"You can," Teague said, nodding. "But that's a miserable way to live."

"Miserable way to live?" She gave him a disbelieving look. "Have you seen your kitchen? That's a miserable way to live."

Teague snorted. "We'll renovate it when we have the time. Sam doesn't need to worry about it right now, and I've been busy setting the sanctuary up."

"Henry said your boyfriend was pregnant." Audrey sighed. "I suppose I can take care of the kitchen for you. Let me know your budget and I'll start."

Teague blinked. "Wait. What happened to being spiteful?"

Audrey arched a brow. "I'm still debating it. Now, when are you going to marry Sam?"

"Hey now, marriage isn't right for every couple, so you shouldn't pressure people into something just because it's more socially acceptable."

Audrey gave him a look. "Okay. *Are* you going to marry Sam?"

Teague shrugged, feeling his cheeks flush. "I haven't found a ring I like yet. It's harder than you would think, and Puff and Tortellini are shit shoppers."

"Puff and Tortellini?"

"My bearded dragon and tortoise. They stay in their terrariums mostly since it's so cold. Shopping for a ring is our bonding time."

Audrey looked up. "My god, he shops with reptiles. Why would this Sam even want to marry him?"

"Excuse me?" Teague arched a brow.

She held a hand up. "I'll take care of it. I'm starting to understand why Henry is still here. It's hard to turn your back on the less fortunate, and you need all the help you can get."

"Be still my beating heart," Teague said dryly.

Audrey ignored him and gave him a curious look. "Do

you really think Timothy and my dad are happy? I spend more time at Papa's house than theirs."

"I know they are." Teague shrugged. "I only see them seven or eight times a year, but I know they're happy together, and my dad deserves that. So does yours."

"Maybe you're right." Audrey bit her lip. "Papa is much happier with Rinaldo too. I think there's just a lot of bitterness left over from the divorce."

"Yeah, you don't want to hear my dad talk about my alpha father." Teague scratched Rollo's neck. "There's no love lost there, and it's impossible for him to be impartial."

Audrey nodded sharply. "Alright. I'll give Dad a chance to explain everything, and I'll help you renovate your home. I could use a new project anyway."

"Gee, thanks. There's a nice bed and breakfast in town."

"Sam said you have an empty guest room." She smiled sweetly. "I'll just stay there for now."

CHAPTER 17

Sam leaned into Teague's side on the porch swing and nipped at his ear. "Why are your stepsiblings living with us? Don't they have trust funds and apartments in New York?"

"I'm going to be honest here," Teague said, scowling. "I have no idea what the fuck is going on with them."

Sam hummed under his breath and cuddled closer. He would never tell him, because he'd get a big head, but Sam loved Teague's scowls and general grumpiness. It was freaking adorable and didn't happen as often anymore. *Guess I can't be mad that my alpha is happy*, he thought with a giggle.

Teague gave him a fond look. "You and Henry get along."

"I taught him how to create a budget." Sam made a face. "He's twenty-two and has no practical life skills."

"He loves Journey," Teague pointed out.

Sam smiled at the reminder. "Okay, so I really do like him."

Henry was currently toting Journey around in a pooch pouch as he walked toward the goat barn. The younger omega really liked animals and seemed happy helping

Teague take care of them. If Sam was honest with himself, he'd admit that he really liked having Teague's stepsiblings there. It felt like they were family, and Sam loved it.

He had plenty of friends in Hobson Hills and was especially close to Reuben and Justin, but it was still nice to have an annoying younger brother and a snotty older sister.

"I still think you did something to Henry's mind." Audrey was wrapped up in a heated blanket with Aunt Mia on the patio bench across the porch. "Why would he want to even be near a goat?" She held up her phone. "What do you think of these cabinets, Aunt Mia?"

Sam chuckled when his aunt squinted at the phone through her reading glasses. He knew she had zero interest in renovations. That was the only reason she hadn't done it a long time ago. Audrey, however, seemed to enjoy asking her opinion on everything.

"I like that butcher block with the white cabinets," Mia said, scratching Merle's ears.

"Very country chic." Audrey's tongue poked out as she pressed something on her phone. "Imagine this layout with those cabinets."

"We're really letting her remodel the kitchen?" Sam asked.

"Do you want to do all that work?" Teague asked, brow raised. "I like watching renovation shows with you, but that shit is hard in real life."

Sam patted his slowly expanding belly. "You make a good point. I'm feeling the need for a trip to Zoe's."

Teague helped Sam stand, then dipped his head to place a warm kiss on his lips. "I live to serve your every whim."

"Oh, well in that case," Sam said, grinning. "Get your ass to our bed."

Aunt Mia laughed and Audrey made a face.

Teague shrugged. "I guess that means no apple-cider muffins."

"Wait now." Sam held his hand up. "Let's not be too hasty. Grab the dogs and let's go to Zoe's. You can pleasure me later."

Mia cackled. "That's my boy."

Sam followed Teague into the house and hunted up all the dog leashes, except for Merle's of course. There was no question that he'd stay home with Aunt Mia. It took them a little time to get everyone bundled up and in the car.

Sam watched the snow-covered pasture pass them by as Teague drove to town. It wasn't so long ago that Sam would have hopped in his car and been at Zoe's by now, but dogs, boyfriends, and a shrinking bladder made things a little more complicated. *Complicated isn't bad*, he thought with a smile.

"I wish Puff could have come with us." Sam looked over his shoulder at the four happily panting dogs. "I bet he gets lonely in his terrarium all winter."

"Nah, Tortellini and he have all kinds of parties while the rest of us are out in the snow." Teague grinned and Sam's heart beat a little faster. Maybe grumpy Teague wasn't the most adorable thing ever.

After parking, they unloaded the dogs and took them to the bookstore. Yeo had taken a liking to them and liked to dog sit when they were at Zoe's.

Yeo ignored them and gave each dog a kiss. "Hi Lily. Hi Moose. Hi Percy. Hi Nugget. How are my sweet puppies?"

"Gee, it's nice to see you too." Sam eyed the extremely pregnant man. *That's going to me in a few months*, he thought, confused at the happiness he felt at the idea. Sometimes it was still hard to imagine a baby growing inside him.

Yeo gave him a hug and shoved him toward the bakery. "Go enjoy yourself. I have puppies to spoil."

"I think Yeo's going to get a dog for Christmas. He seems awfully fond of ours." Teague held his hand as they walked into the bakery. Christmas was only a couple of weeks away, so Main Street was busy with shoppers and the normal Saturday-afternoon traffic.

They had just sat at their favorite booth when a man strode into the bakery and glared at Teague. Sam didn't recognize the alpha. He was tall and broad-shouldered and dressed in a business suit. He wore black-framed glasses and had familiar-looking eyes.

Teague groaned. "Damn it, we just want some muffins."

"We need to talk," the man said. "Now."

Teague gave Sam an apologetic look. "Sam, this is Sterling, Dennis's eldest. Sterling, this is my boyfriend, Sam."

"This is Zoe's bakery." Sam gestured around them. "I'll let you buy me some muffins and you can tell us all about how you think Timothy is screwing Dennis out of a fortune or whatever."

Sterling gave him a flat look. "What kind do you want?"

Sam blinked, surprised at the alpha's capitulation. "Oh, uh, three apple-cider muffins and one banana nut." He looked at Teague. "What do you want?"

"You won't share?" Teague asked with a small smile.

"Uh, no. I love you, but these are muffins."

A few moments later, Sterling sat across from them and slid a plate of muffins and a mug of warm milk in front of Sam.

"Thanks." Sam focused on his muffins and did his best to ignore the two men. Unfortunately, they insisted on talking.

"What did you do to Henry and Audrey?" Sterling asked, getting straight to the point. "They were upset about Dad changing his will and came here. Now, they're suddenly happy country folk?"

"I wouldn't say Audrey is happy," Teague said, rubbing his chin. "I think she's suspicious and is waiting for me to do something. I don't know what that something is, but here we are."

"Henry likes animals." Sam licked a crumb from the corner of his mouth. "Why didn't he have any pets before? He wouldn't answer me when I asked him."

"Papa doesn't like animals," Sterling said, watching him coldly. "They're messy and spread diseases."

Sam frowned. *Brett doesn't like animals either.*

"Well, Henry has a dog now, so get used to it." Teague glared at Sterling. "He's twenty-two and has his own home."

Sterling shrugged. "I don't care if he has a dog. I care that you've somehow convinced my sister and brother that your omega dad isn't using *our* father for his money."

Teague groaned, head falling back. "Why is it the same shit all the time?" He gave Sterling a hard look. "Talk to Dennis about this shit theory of yours and get over it."

"I did," Sterling said, gritting his teeth. "He says he's *in love.*"

Sam waved his hand and took another bite of his muffin. "There you go. Answer given."

Sterling arched a brow. "*Love* is nature's way of tricking people into reproducing. It's not a real answer."

Sam gave the alpha a sympathetic look. "You poor foolish man." He elbowed Teague. "It's like he's begging us to find him someone to love. So, how long are you going to be in town, Sterling?"

He could ask Henry what Sterling's preferences were and start a list as soon as they got home. *Ah, having family is great.*

Sterling gave him a horrified look. "Don't even think about it."

"Too late." Teague grinned. "That's his thinking face. He's already making plans. We'll have you matched up by the end of next year. Are you monogamous or polyamorous?"

Sterling stood. "I'm going back to your house. Aunt Mia is far more sensible than the two of you."

"You can stay in the hamsters' room, but they run on their

wheels all night," Sam said, and took a large bite of his last muffin.

Sterling didn't answer. He just turned and walked away.

"I'm glad our house has a lot of rooms." Teague sighed. "Are you mad that they're here. I'm sorry they keep showing up."

Sam hugged Teague and sneaked a piece of his muffin. "I think they're your family whether you like it or not."

Teague gave him a look. "So, this probably isn't the best time, but I have a question for you."

Sam sipped his milk. "Okay."

Teague pulled a small box out of his pocket and opened it. Inside was a rose-gold band covered in brown diamond beads. "I love you, Sammie. Nothing else in my life has ever felt more right, than having you by my side. Please, do me the honor of marrying me."

Sam stared at the beautiful ring, mouth opening and closing. *Teague wants to marry me.*

After the extended silence, Teague gave him an agonized look and closed the box. "I'm stupid, aren't I? Of course, it's too soon for you to want to marry me."

Sam growled and grabbed the ring box before Teague could put it in his pocket. "Mine."

Teague gave him a confused look. "Sam?"

"You're mine too." Sam swallowed hard. "You're my family and my home, Teague. Of course, I'll marry you. Now, put this beautiful ring on my finger."

Teague grinned. "You'll have to let me hold the box."

Sam flushed and slid the box back to him. "Sorry."

"Audrey helped me pick it out. I've had to carry it with me, because Morris kept trying to steal it. I think he wanted to propose to you."

Sam covered his heart. "I would have said yes."

Teague laughed and slid the ring onto Sam's finger. "I swear, Sam. I will do my best to be the man you need."

Sam cupped his face. "You already are, you idiot."

Teague kissed him, lips parting and tongue moving with his. Sam thought he could live the rest of his life on Teague's kisses alone.

"Seriously? Don't you all have a house or something?" a familiar voice said.

Sam leaned back and blinked up at Judd, the alpha he and Teague had gone on a date with. "I'm engaged."

Judd grinned. "Congratulations. I'm hoping you're engaged to the man you're kissing. Otherwise, you've just crushed my belief in love."

Sam snorted. "Yeah. Teague is an even better fiancé than he is a best friend. Sorry, you missed your shot at all of this." He gestured down his body. "Better luck next time."

Judd laughed again and waved at their empty cups. "Let me buy you some drinks to congratulate you two."

Teague smirked and wrapped his arm around Sam's shoulders. "That sounds perfect."

CHAPTER 18

Teague paced back and forth across the living room floor, Binks nestled on his head. "Are we sure it was a good idea to send Sterling to pick them up at the airport?"

"Yes," Audrey said, eyes glued to her phone. "I'm tired of hearing him complain about Barnaby and Leroy. He knew they liked their wheels when he decided to stay here."

Noodle curled in Audrey's lap and gave them her normal, imperious look. It looked scarily similar to Audrey's own expression.

Sam and Henry giggled about something. They were decorating the tree that stood in front of the big picture window. Morris had already called dibs to the top of the tree.

Teague bent and picked up Charlie for a cuddle. As usual, the cat's purrs calmed him. "What if he tries to break them up?"

Mia snorted and adjusted the blanket lying across her legs. "I know the man is like the grim reaper of love, but if he hasn't managed to talk those two into a breakup yet, what makes you think he will now?"

Audrey chuckled. "The grim reaper of love. I like that. That so fits him."

"I don't know why I'm so nervous." Teague sat down, and Moose jumped onto the couch to lie across him and Charlie.

Teague really *did* know why he was so nervous. Dennis had put *Teague* in his will. Dennis considered him one of his kids.

Mia gave him a knowing look. "Calm your ass down, Tee."

The knock at the door had him standing quickly, dumping both Charlie and Moose from his lap. He rushed to answer it, then frowned when he saw Reuben. "Oh, it's you."

"Teague," Sam chided, hip bumping him out of the doorway. "Why are you so rude to my favorite person in the whole world?"

"You brought him cookies, didn't you?" Teague asked, amused.

Reuben's eyes danced with laughter when he smiled. "Yep."

"You're the best, Reuben. I owe you one." Sam grabbed the box the other man held and ran back to Henry. "I got them! These are the *best* Christmas cookies you will ever eat."

Teague smiled at Reuben. "I'm sorry he's a pig. Do you want to come in? We have eggnog."

Reuben looked a little panicked at the idea. "No. Thanks though. I was just dropping the cookies off on the way home."

Teague's eyes widened when he saw Sterling's rental pull into the driveway. "Shit, they're here."

Reuben looked over his shoulder. "I better get going. I hope you have a good time with your dads."

He left before Teague could correct him. *My dads.*

Timothy and Dennis were both tanned, relaxed, and happy. "It's so cold," Timothy said, hugging Teague. "I miss the sun, but I missed your face more." He stepped back and smiled wide. "So, I hear congratulations are in order?"

Teague glared at Sterling.

The other alpha blinked a few times and shrugged. "I didn't realize it was a secret."

Timothy gave them a serene look. "I'm going to be a father-in-law and a grandpa both. I love it."

Dennis grinned and patted Teague's shoulder. "Congratulations, Teague. I was surprised to see Sterling at the airport, but he explained that the kids are all staying here for the holidays. It'll be the first Christmas I've had all the kids together since the divorce. Thank you for talking them into it."

"I didn't." Teague sighed. "They just won't leave."

Audrey waved from the couch. "Hello, Dad. Ignore Teague. He loves us. Oh, go look at the kitchen. I remodeled it for them for Christmas."

Dennis bent and kissed her head. "Hello, sweetheart. I'm surprised you're not in Aspen for the holidays."

She shrugged and looked back at her phone, her cheeks pinkening. "Obviously, Teague and Sam needed my help with the house. I'll be doing the guestrooms next. I'm currently staying in the reptile room, but Puff and Tortellini are good roommates. They just need a style makeover."

Dennis's eyes softened. "They're lucky to have you, baby girl."

"Hey, Dad." Henry rushed over and hugged Dennis. "Meet Journey, your grand-pooch."

Dennis laughed and patted Journey's head. The dog practically lived in Henry's pooch pouch. "I didn't know you liked animals, son. Journey is one of Teague's rescues, isn't he?"

"He was, but now he's mine." Henry bounced in place. "Oh, and Sam helped me set up a budget, so I don't need to borrow money for Christmas."

Dennis's mouth fell open. "You don't?"

"Nope." Henry grinned and moved on to hug Timothy. "It's good to see you too. Your son's fiancé is the absolute best. Just so you know."

Timothy startled, surprised at the hug, but squeezed Henry back. "Sam is a darling, isn't he? I'm so glad you can be here with us this year."

"Me too." Henry ducked his head. "Papa and Rinaldo are in Paris for the holidays. I didn't think they would want a third wheel."

Timothy rolled his eyes. "The holidays aren't supposed to be romantic. They're supposed to be hectic, stressful, and full of family." He eyed the gathering herd of dogs and pigs. "And pets, because where Teague lives, pets live."

"Have a cookie." Sam held out the container of cookies. His cheeks were puffed out, and he wore a look of bliss on his face that Teague was very familiar with.

Teague grabbed one of the cookies and bit into it. He moaned. *So damn good.*

Sterling nudged his shoulder and pushed him a little closer to Dennis. "Dad, you wanted to tell Teague something, remember?"

Dennis flushed and looked shy for a moment before his normal confidence returned. "Ah, yes. Sterling explained some of his concerns over the changes in my will." He narrowed his eyes on Audrey. "I'll be seeing to it that there aren't any more leaks in my lawyer's office."

Audrey shrugged. "Just don't fire his paralegal. My personal trainer will be devastated."

Dennis shook his head. "Anyway, I made it clear to Sterling that you're my son now. I love you and I'll be leaving you any damn thing I want when I die. That's my prerogative, and anyone who doesn't like it can just get over it."

Teague's eyes watered, and he blinked rapidly. "Thank you, sir. It means a lot to me to have you for a dad."

Timothy's lip trembled. "Oh, lord, this is just perfect."

Aunt Mia cleared her throat. "Why don't you all have a seat, and Sam will share his cookies with everyone?"

Sam glared at Mia. "Fine."

Teague sat down, and Sam slid onto his lap. His omega nuzzled behind his ear. "I love you, Tee. Look at our family. This is going to be the best Christmas ever."

CHAPTER 19

*S*am stared at his huge baby bump in the mirror. "Why the hell didn't we wait until after the baby was born to do this?"

Mia chuckled from where she sat nearby. She wore a lovely light-blue dress and warm white shawl. "You were the one that wanted to have the wedding *before* Casey was born."

"You look handsome," Justin said, patting his shoulder and grinning at him in the mirror. "Plus, believe me, you won't have time to worry about a wedding once you have a newborn to take care of."

Sam gave himself a doubtful look. He wore a pair of gray slacks, a white paternity dress shirt, and a gray suit jacket that wouldn't button. A boutonniere of white and blue flowers that he couldn't name was pinned to his collar.

"You look good," Reuben said, deep voice soothing.

"Are you sure you're okay with being a groomsman?" Sam gave his friend a concerned look. Reuben had a handle on his social anxiety, but he had good days and bad days. Sam didn't want to be the reason for a bad day.

Reuben straightened out his light-blue suit jacket. "I look too good to back out."

Sam grinned. "You sure do. Ernie was eying you earlier."

Justin snorted. "Ernie eyes him all the time."

"Hey, Sam." Henry shut the door behind him and leaned against it. Sam's final groomsman looked pretty nice himself, even if he did have Journey in a gray pooch pouch to match his suit. Sam couldn't argue much. Morris was going to walk with him down the aisle.

"What's up?" he asked, turning back to the mirror and checking his hair.

"There's a man here asking to talk to you in private." Henry bit his lip. "I don't like him."

"It's probably the florist." Sam shrugged. "I'm as good as I'm going to get anyway. Will you help Reuben with his boutonniere?"

"Sure." Henry smiled shyly at Reuben. The omega was an odd combination of arrogance and shyness.

Sam slipped out of the dressing room and looked around. They had decided to have the wedding at an event barn close to the house. One of Gramps Wilson's sons owned it, so they got a discount.

The place looked beautiful thanks to Audrey and Mia. The two had taken over planning the wedding when neither Sam nor Teague had shown any interest in it. *I just want my Tee*, he thought, smiling. *Today I get him.*

His smile faded when he saw Brett. The alpha moved to stand in front of him, eyes calculating.

"You're pregnant." Brett looked him up and down. "You look good, even with the weight."

Sam rolled his eyes and tugged at his shirt self-consciously. "Why did I waste years on you?"

Brett's face flushed and he grabbed Sam's hands. "I flew all the way out to the middle of nowhere to talk since you won't answer my calls or texts. Sam, you don't belong with Teague. You and I are meant to be together. I'll even accept the baby. Let's go home."

The surrealness of the moment amazed him. A year ago, he would have given anything to hear those words from Brett. *Damn, that makes me sad.*

Sam pulled his hands out of Brett's. "You're a selfish, narcissistic asshole Brett. That's always been true, and I wish that I had seen it a hell of a lot sooner. We will *never* be together again."

Brett scowled and crossed his arms. "I knew Teague wanted you, and now he's filled your head with nonsense."

Sam's eyes narrowed. "Teague actually has nothing to do with it. My head is full of my own thoughts and ideas, thank you very much. I'm not some confused little omega who is just waiting for some alpha to step in and tell me how to feel. I deserve better than you. I deserve a man that knows and respects me. One that appreciates who I am as a person. Even if I wasn't in love with Teague, you wouldn't be that person."

Brett gave him a disbelieving look. "You're turning *me* down?"

Sam gave him a flat look. "Go away. I don't want your alphaholeness to corrupt my wedding."

Brett moved closer, eyes heating. "You don't know what you're saying."

"Excuse me, young man," Gramps Wilson said, grabbing one of Brett's shoulders. "I think you need to leave like Sam told you to."

Doc Grover tugged on Brett's other arm. "Let us just help you to the door."

"Let go of me, old man," Brett shrugged off Gramps and Grover's grips. "I'm not going anywhere without my omega."

Gramps's smile was a little scary. "Sam, go on back inside

the dressing room and finish getting ready. We'll take care of this for you."

Grover snickered and grabbed Brett again, this time with a stronger grip. "You look nice, Sam. Go on inside."

Sam smirked. "Goodbye Brett. I don't even care if Gramps hides your body somewhere in the woods. I'm so done with you."

"Damn it," someone said from behind them. "Why do people always have to say things like that where I can hear them?"

Sam turned around. "Oh, hi there, Sheriff McKenzie." He smiled widely and waved. "Lovely day for a wedding, isn't it?"

"It's snowing." The handsome older alpha looked the three of them over. "What's going on here?"

"Removing a wedding crasher." Gramps grinned. "Come on, Mack. Help us get this shithead out of Sam's hair."

"I will, but no hiding bodies." Sheriff McKenzie paused. "What am I saying? No killing anyone."

"You're *killing* our joy," Grover mumbled under his breath.

Sam chuckled and went back inside the dressing room.

"Problems, tater tot?" Aunt Mia asked.

Sam smiled, feeling lighter than he had in a really long time. "I'm pretty great, aren't I?"

Reuben nodded. "Yep."

Sam clapped his hands. "Let's get this wedding over, so I can get my man to our honeymoon cabin."

Since Sam wasn't keen on traveling far while seven months pregnant, they were spending a week by themselves in Reuben's small cabin in the woods. Justin and his family were even staying at the house with Aunt Mia and the pets while they were gone, and Doc Grover, Henry, and Hannah were going to take care of the animal sanctuary.

Their wedding planner, Barry Lawson, watched him from the doorway, arms crossed. "My thoughts exactly. We're about to start, so I'll let you know when Teague's party has made it down the aisle."

"Thanks." Sam smiled, not even ashamed at his eagerness. He wanted wedding cake and Teague. That was it.

A few moments later, Barry started waving them out of the room.

"Time to get you married, Sam." Justin straightened his jacket and took Nugget's leash. The golden retriever wore a light blue top hat today.

Sam heard "When I fall in Love" playing as the door opened, and suddenly realized it was happening. *I'm getting married.*

Justin left and a moment later, Barry waved to Reuben.

Reuben picked up Charlie. The black cat looked handsome with a light blue bowtie around his neck. Reuben paused at the door and pulled Sam into a hug. "I'm happy for you."

Sam hugged his friend back. "I am too. Thanks for being here, Reuben. Also, thanks for that delicious-looking cake."

His friend had made the wedding cake. Sam and Teague had loved the blackberry and curd buttercream cake, and Reuben had created a beautiful, rustic woodland design with blackberries on top and little paw prints making a path around all three tiers. He had even made several cupcakes with their many pets' faces frosted onto them. Sam had eaten a Niles cupcake earlier and loved the lemony goodness.

"Anything for a friend." Reuben patted his back and left.

Henry fetched Niles and cooed over the cat's little gray tux. "Such a cutie."

Sam shook his head, still somewhat amazed that he'd become friends with the omega.

Henry gave him a wink and left the room when Barry gestured him out.

Aunt Mia stood up and settled Merle on the floor. She gave Sam a fond look. "I'm proud of you, sweet pea."

Sam hugged her. "You're proud that Teague and I finally realized what was right under our noses?"

She chuckled, her thin body shaking with her laughter. "That's for sure. I'm also proud that you've learned your own value. I heard what you told Brett. All of us eavesdropped." She patted his cheek. "You are such a joy to me and everyone who knows you. You deserve only the best, and I'm proud of you for going after it."

He swallowed hard and hugged her tightly. "I love you, Aunt Mia."

"I love you too, donut hole."

He scowled and pushed away from her. "I don't love that term of endearment."

Mia snickered and tugged him toward the door. "That's why I use it. Grab your bird. I believe Morris thinks you're marrying him."

Sam fetched his bird and perched the parrot on his right arm. "I love you, Morris."

"Love you, beautiful." Morris preened and fluffed up his feathers.

Sam grinned and left the room.

Mia took his left arm and when Barry motioned them forward, they began the short trip down the aisle.

Sam sniffled. For some reason he was surprised everyone they had invited had come. He knew he had friends, but it did something to him to see them show up for Teague and him. For so long, it had just been Sam, Mia, and Teague. Now, he had a bigger family than he realized.

Audrey, Sterling, and Doc Grover stood with their own pet entourage next to the wedding officiary.

Sam chuckled. All the pets except Puff and Tortellini were there. It was a little too cold for the bearded dragon and tortoise to be out and about.

Then Sam saw his alpha and he couldn't seem to focus on anyone else. Teague stood tall and straight in front of the wedding officiary. Binks nestled on his head and watched them expectantly.

When Teague saw him, his serious expression shifted and he grinned, his eyes lighting up.

"You do that to him," Aunt Mia whispered. "You make him smile."

Sam shivered. "He makes me smile too."

Aunt Mia leaned up and kissed his cheek before handing him off to Teague and finding her seat next to Timothy and Dennis.

The rest of the ceremony went by quickly. Sam stuttered over his vows, but Teague's eyes on him told Sam it didn't matter. Morris said his own vows of love as Binks made his eerily good meow sounds. Sam was a little jealous because Morris's were simple but good.

"Love you, love you, love you," Morris repeated.

The woman performing the ceremony smiled. "I now pronounce you married."

Sam handed Morris to Henry, then happily kissed Teague. He couldn't wait to see where life brought them.

CHAPTER 20

THREE MONTHS LATER

Teague smoothed a finger down Casey's soft, round cheek. The baby was so tiny and perfect with light-brown skin and warm-brown hair. His omega son was going to look just like him. At least that's what Sam said.

Casey waved a fist in the air and took a deep breath, working his way up to a cry.

Teague took him from the bassinet and cuddled him close. "You need a new diaper, tater tot."

A light laugh came from behind him and he turned around.

Sam grinned at him. "You and Aunt Mia have already started with the weird nicknames."

Teague shrugged and took Casey to the changing table. "Mia is a bad influence on me."

Sam nodded in agreement, then yawned. He sat in one of the white rocking chairs next to the bay window. "Who knew how exhausting having a baby would be?"

"Everyone." Teague nodded at Casey. "Everyone told us we were going to have a rough few months."

Charlie hopped onto Sam's lap and snuggled in close. Both Charlie and Niles practically lived in the nursery with Casey. They even had their own cat tree in between the rocking chairs. Niles currently curled into a ball on his favorite blanket pile on the tree.

Sam scratched Charlie's back and reached over to pet Niles. "Nanny cats."

Teague snapped Casey's fresh onesie in place and cuddled him close again. He stepped over Lily and Nugget and settled into the second rocking chair.

Audrey and Aunt Mia had decorated the nursery in soft whites and greens. Illustrations of baby animals covered the walls and knitted stuffies filled the corner shelf. Reuben's husband, Ernie, was a knitter and spoiled Casey and all the pets with blankets, stuffies, and clothes.

It didn't take long for Casey to fall back asleep, so Teague settled him back into the bassinet. He looked over and chuckled when he noticed Sam was also asleep. Neither of them had gotten much rest in the past month, so a nap sounded good.

Teague picked Charlie up and settled a blanket around his omega before returning the cat to his napping spot on Sam's lap.

He slipped out of the nursery and headed downstairs to the kitchen. Audrey and Aunt Mia had done a beautiful job there too. The seventies' nightmare had been transformed into a simple and cozy kitchen with new tiled floors, butcher-block counters, and white cabinets.

Aunt Mia sat in her favorite rocking chair near the window with Merle at her feet and Dove curled on her lap.

She smiled. "How's it going up there?"

"Casey and Sam are both asleep." Teague yawned and poured himself a cup of coffee.

"You two need more rest." She gave him a stubborn look. "You could move Casey's bassinet into my room."

Teague shook his head. Mia still tired out easily, and they didn't want her to overdo it. "Dad and Dennis are coming over next weekend to take baby duty, and Audrey said something about coming to visit her favorite niece in a few weeks."

"Was she talking about Casey or Noodle?" Mia said, arching a brow.

Teague laughed. "I really don't know."

Henry whistled as he came in through the back door. "Hey, the sanctuary animals all have their breakfasts and I gathered some eggs."

Teague gave his stepbrother a grateful smile and sat at the kitchen table. "Thanks. I don't know what I would have done without you here this month."

Henry shrugged and gave him a shy look. "Gramps Wilson said there was a house for sale down the road. I was thinking of maybe getting it and having it fixed up. It would be nice to have my own place when I visit, and Dad and Timothy could even use it when they come."

Teague gave him a considering look. "Audrey and Sterling couldn't use it too?"

Henry shook his head. "Nope. They can stay in your attic."

"Gee, thanks." Teague laughed. "Really, though, I love having you nearby. Sam does too."

Henry nodded. "Sam helped me figure out how the purchase will fit in my budget."

Teague wasn't surprised, since Sam had taken Henry under his wing. Teague was a little ashamed to say that he wouldn't have bothered giving Henry much thought or time if Sam hadn't become the other omega's friend. Henry's issues with Timothy and Dennis were a little complicated, but at least Teague wasn't in the middle of it anymore.

Henry set Journey down, so the dog could play with the others, then followed Orville and Wilbur into the living room.

Aunt Mia smiled at him over her cup as she sipped her coffee.

"What are you smiling at?" Teague asked, giving her a fond look.

"I remember when you first video called me." She chuckled. "Binks sat in your hair, and you had the dourest expression. I asked about your family and you said it was just you and your dad."

Teague shrugged, confused. "Yeah?"

"Look at you now," she said, shaking her head. "Here you sit with *two* dads, a sister, two brothers, a great-aunt, a husband, and a baby. You and Sam both are overloaded with family."

Teague blinked a few times and looked around. Several of his pets spread out on the floor. Casey's baby swing sat next to Mia's rocking chair. Henry's favorite coffee cup sat in the sink, and a covered plate of cookies sat on the counter. Sam had been in a baking mood yesterday.

Loving animals as much as he did, it was a long time since Teague's house had been empty, but it had still been lonely. Now, there was no room for loneliness.

"I have a pretty good life," he said.

"It's only possible because you took a chance." Mia set her cup on the windowsill and stroked Dove's back. "I'm proud of you boys for throwing in together and building a life. I'm going to enjoy watching you two get into trouble together."

"For years to come." Teague blinked back tears. He was completely blaming the exhaustion for his sentimentality this morning.

Mia nodded and stood up slowly. She set Dove down and pulled her shawl closer around her. "Now, if you'll excuse me, I'm having breakfast with George Spencer. He'll be picking me up anytime now. I may just get lucky by lunch."

Teague winced at the image now firmly planted in his brain. "Have fun."

He finished his coffee and went back upstairs with a bucket of vegetables. Audrey called Puff and Tortellini's room The Reptile Room, and had taken great joy in decorating it in warm browns and dark greens.

Puff's three-tier corner terrarium dominated one side of the room. The bearded dragon was currently snuggled up with his yellow toy lizard. He was a little worn out from his trip to Yeo's bookstore yesterday. The omega's son had a friend with another bearded dragon named Pudding, so Puff and Pudding had spent the day having a costume photoshoot.

"Poor tired dragon." Teague quickly put together Puff's breakfast from the vegetables he had brought up and set it in his enclosure.

Tortellini's terrarium stretched under the double windows of the room. Teague had to move Mimi from the top before he could set the tortoise's breakfast inside.

Mimi meowed pitifully.

Teague rolled his eyes. "He'll come out and play after breakfast. Try walking around on your own instead of waiting to ride him."

A warm chuckle sounded behind him, sending a shiver down his back.

Sam stood in the doorway, eyes sleepy. "I already fed and watered Barnaby and Leroy."

Teague pulled him into a hug. "Thanks, beautiful."

Sam settled his head on Teague's shoulder. "I love you."

"Love you too." Teague's voice was gruff even to his own ears.

Aunt Mia's earlier words still echoed in his mind. In Sam, he had found a partner and lover to stand beside him through anything. He had found his home.

BOOKS BY C.W. GRAY

Writing as C.W. Gray

- **Charybdis Station Chronicles** – *science fiction/fantasy, mpreg*

The Blue Solace Series
The Mercenary's Mate
The General's Mate
The Soldier's Mate
The Lieutenant's Mate
The Engineer's Mate
The Captain's Mate
The Rebel's Mate
Charybdis Station
Death's Mate
Fire's Mate
Rune and Silas – Coming Soon

- **The Hobson Hills Omegas** – non-shifter, mpreg, omegaverse

Falling for the Omega
Snow Kisses for My Omega
"The Beta's Love Song"
Romancing the Omega
"Bennett's Dream"
Healing the Omega
"Justin's Journey"
A Pint for my Omega
Unraveling the Omega
"Grey's Gift"
Hobson Hills Shorts: Volume One
"Zoe's Happily Ever After"
The Alpha's Christmas Wish
Convincing the Alpha
Loving My Omega
The Sheriff's Omega (McKenzie's book) – Coming Soon
Admiring his Omega (Cain's book) – Coming Soon

- **Holiday Omegas Shorts** – holiday short stories from the world of The Silver Isles – paranormal, mpreg, omegaverse

"Cauldron Cake Pops and a Witch's Kiss"
"Sugar Cookies and a Witch's Love"
"Candy Hearts and a Witch's Ring"
"Carrot Cake and a Witch's Surprise"
Sonny and Leo (Anthology with books 1-4)
Muddy Paws and a Fae's Wings – *Coming in October 2020*

- **The Silver Isles** – paranormal, mermen, mpreg, omegaverse

The Guppy Prince
The Not so Little Merman

"A Mate from the Deep"
The Sea Witch – Coming Soon
Writing as Chloe Gray

- **A Little Bit of Perfect** – contemporary, non-mpreg, Daddy/Little age play

Adler and Orrick

Tobias and Beau – Coming Soon

If you would like to keep up with releases, please like and follow me on my Facebook author page, join C.W. Gray's Reading Nook on Facebook, or visit my website at (https://www.cwgray-author.com).

www.ingramcontent.com/pod-product-compliance
Lightning Source LLC
Chambersburg PA
CBHW050002040726
47599CB00014B/1177